The Evolution of Inanimate Objects

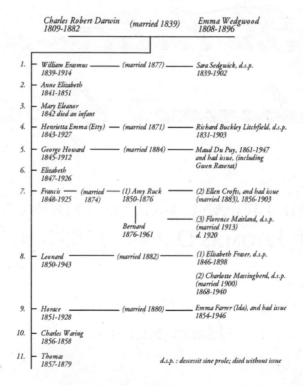

Charles Robert Darwin 1809-1882	(married 1839)	Emma Wedgwood 1808-1896

1. — William Erasmus —— (married 1877) —— Sara Sedgwick, d.s.p.
   1839-1914   1839-1902

2. — Anne Elizabeth
   1841-1851

3. — Mary Eleanor
   1842 died an infant

4. — Henrietta Emma (Etty) —— (married 1871) —— Richard Buckley Litchfield, d.s.p.
   1843-1927   1831-1903

5. — George Howard —————— (married 1884) —— Maud Du Puy, 1861-1947
   1845-1912   and had issue, (including
                                             Gwen Raverat)

6. — Elizabeth
   1847-1926

7. — Francis —— (married —— (1) Amy Ruck   (2) Ellen Crofts, and had issue
   1848-1925   1874)   1850-1876   (married 1883), 1856-1903

                                               (3) Florence Maitland, d.s.p.
                             Bernard   (married 1913)
                             1876-1961   d. 1920

8. — Leonard —————————— (married 1882) —— (1) Elisabeth Fraser, d.s.p.
   1850-1943   1846-1898

                                            (2) Charlotte Massingberd, d.s.p.
                                            (married 1900)
                                            1868-1940

9. — Horace ————————— (married 1880) —— Emma Farrer (Ida), and had issue
   1851-1928   1854-1946

10. — Charles Waring
    1856-1858

11. — Thomas
    1857-1879   d.s.p. : descessit sine prole; died without issue

Frontispiece: The Darwin Family Tree

The Evolution of Inanimate Objects

THE LIFE AND COLLECTED WORKS OF THOMAS DARWIN (1857-1879)

A NOVEL BY

Harry Karlinsky

The Friday Project
An imprint of HarperCollins*Publishers*
77–85 Fulham Palace Road
Hammersmith, London W6 8JB
www.harpercollins.co.uk

First published in Great Britain by The Friday Project in 2012

A catalogue record for this book is
available from the British Library

ISBN 978-0-00-745435-8

Printed and bound in Great Britain by
Clays Ltd, St Ives plc

MIX
Paper from
responsible sources
FSC www.fsc.org FSC™ C007454

For Sally, Franny, April, and Elizabeth

He who will go thus far, ought not to hesitate to go one step further
— Charles Darwin, *On the Origin of Species*

A world of made is not a world of born
— e. e. cummings, *Complete Poems*, 1904–1962

CONTENTS

PREFACE

This work was intended to be a treatise on the history of Canadian asylums, particularly the London Asylum, which was among the first Canadian facilities established for the care of the insane. Opened in 1870 three miles east (at the time) of the city of London, Ontario, by 1879 more than 700 patients were lodged — a word chosen carefully — within its imposing structure. Regrettably, detailed descriptions of the initial patients and their illnesses are virtually nonexistent. Although casebooks, now housed in the Archives of the Province of Ontario, were maintained throughout each patient's stay, the most consistent entries at the time of admission were limited to the patient's name, sex, age, religion, birthplace, occupation, and civil condition (whether single, married, or widowed). Additional notes describing a patient's symptoms or circumstances prior to admission were rare.

Sadly, "scant though this admitting information was, it was far more than was usually recorded later in the patient's career."[1] *Career* was an apt word. The majority of those admitted to the London Asylum did not recover and receded quietly into the anonymity of institutional life. Most commonly, subsequent documentation was confined to brief annual notes to the effect that a patient's clinical status had remained unchanged. Only dramatic and untoward events altered this singular and uniform rhythm.

My preliminary research included a casebook review of all admissions to the London Asylum during the year 1879. On July 2nd of that year, Thomas Darwin, age twenty-one, was assessed and admitted by Dr. Richard Maurice Bucke, Medical Superintendent. Aside from the dull identifying details referred to above, there were no further clinical observations. Mr. Darwin was a single male of unstated religion and occupation. His birthplace was Down, England. An accompanying, and apparently standard, document issued by the Department of the Provincial Secretary of Ontario authorized transfer of Mr. Darwin from the Toronto Gaol (now better known as the Don Jail), where he had evidently been imprisoned for the previous twelve days as "danger-

---

1. Shortt, S.E.D. *Victorian Lunacy: Richard M. Bucke and the Practice of Late Nineteenth-Century Psychiatry*. Cambridge History of Medicine Series. Cambridge: Cambridge University Press, 1986, p.50. For the sources of subsequent quotations used in this text, readers are referred to the "Sources for Quotations" section that begins on page 200.

ous to others." The only additional entry in Thomas Darwin's casebook was dated just under four months later — "Death due to tuberculosis — October 23rd, 1879. R. M. Bucke."

The surname Darwin aroused my immediate interest. There was Charles Darwin, of course — *the* Charles Darwin — of *On the Origin of Species*. But who was Thomas?

The imperfect story has now emerged.

Thomas Darwin was the last of eleven children born to Charles Robert Darwin and Emma Wedgwood. Scattered details of his early years can be found by focussed reading of obvious sources — primarily the preserved correspondence of Emma Darwin (particularly the letters to her maiden aunt, Fanny Allen) as well as the affectionate but unpolished accounts of Charles Darwin's life by various descendants. The writings of Charles Darwin also contain a number of references to his youngest son. These include his *Autobiography* as well as his text *The Expression of the Emotions in Man and Animals* where descriptions of Thomas appear on three occasions. There are also the "scientific" observations of Thomas's first eighteen months contained within one of his father's unpublished diaries.

Little preserved material relates to Thomas's adolescence or early adulthood. There are the brief annual reports of his student experience at Clapham, a boarding school attended by other members of his family. Accounts of Thomas's subsequent two years at Cambridge University are largely confined to the transcriptions of his readings to the *Plinian Society*, a student group devoted to discourse on the natural sciences, as well as a preserved expense notebook with its list of purchases incurred during Thomas's brief research excursion to Sheffield. There is also Thomas's single letter to his father, and his father's response, both previously published in various compilations of Darwin correspondence. Finally, brief reminiscences of Thomas appear in an acquaintance's memoir.

According to Darwin family lore, an otherwise healthy Thomas tragically and abruptly died of tuberculosis while travelling in Canada following his second year at Cambridge. Essential to the expanded, and surprising, life story presented in this account are two key and previously unappreciated collections of primary sources.

First and foremost, my enquiry into the career of Thomas Darwin's Canadian physician, Richard M. Bucke, led to an assortment of relevant materials now housed in the Rare Book Room at the University of Western Ontario. These include Bucke's diaries, one of which contains a number of entries concerning Thomas's psychiatric illness along with a letter, almost certainly confiscated, that Thomas wrote to his mother near the end of his confinement in the London Asylum. As well, there is the brief correspondence — previously unpublished — between Bucke and Charles Darwin, which includes a short note that Charles Darwin requested Bucke deliver to his son. The collection also includes Bucke's extensive scientific and personal correspondence, including the first draft of a letter he wrote to the physician William Osler concerning Thomas; letters to and from J. W. Langmuir, the province of Ontario's Inspector of Asylums, Prisons, and Public Charities; and of less relevance to this account, notes to and from the poet Walt Whitman. Lastly, two additional documents associated with Thomas's transfer to the London Asylum that were amongst a series of "Admission Warrants and Histories" dating to the early 1870s were a significant find. This material was relocated to the Rare Book Room on the closure of a small archival and teaching museum that had previously been maintained in what is now London's Regional Mental Health Care facility.

The second crucial array of source material revolves around Thomas Darwin's unpublished manuscript submitted to the journal *Nature*. As Charles Darwin's letter to Bucke alluded to this work, I contacted the current administration at *Nature*'s head office in London, England. The article in question (titled, "Hybrid Artefacts and Their Role in Our Understanding of the Evolution of Inanimate Objects") as well as a copy of its letter of rejection was eventually unearthed in an archived file.[2] In what

2. Hurrah, hurrah!

must have been an extraordinary circumstance, Thomas's submission prompted a concerned Joseph Norman Lockyer, the Editor of *Nature* at that time, to write to Charles Darwin. A copy of this letter, as well as Charles Darwin's response, was also preserved in the *Nature* file.

In summary, what was intended to be a (lively!) academic account of Canadian asylums circuitously and with growing momentum has evolved into a biography of Thomas Darwin and a repository for those images, letters, and manuscripts that unfold his story. Chapters 1 to 4 provide a brief sketch of Thomas's life — from his earliest days at Down House, through school days and Cambridge to, finally, his involuntary admission and subsequent death in the London Asylum. Thomas's known scholarly works, all related in some way to his unusual interest in eating utensils, are reproduced in Chapters 5 to 8, along with details of their critical reception. Original source material related to his psychiatric illness and his confinement in the London Asylum is presented in Chapters 9 and 10.

The concluding Epilogue is a contemporary reappraisal of Thomas's scholarly contributions as well as his underlying illness. Thomas Darwin's life merits such resurrection, both as a testament to his significant accomplishments and for the bittersweet depth it adds to our knowledge of Charles Darwin, eminent scientist and devoted father.

[10th October 1879]

[10th October 1879]

To Dr. William Osler
Institutes of Medicine,
McGill University,
Montreal

Dear Will,

I look forward to your imminent arrival. Here in London our committee has been hard at work, and we excitedly await those attending the Annual Meeting. Please note we commence at 10 o'clock on the 16th, and your anatomical demonstration will be the first of two morning presentations. I warn you now that Buller follows you with a talk on pilocarpine in iritis — brace yourself!

And now on to a serious matter. The spread of tuberculosis is a current concern at the Asylum. At present, three of our patients have suspected cases, one of whom is a young man whose condition worries me greatly. His name is Thomas Darwin, the youngest son of England's celebrated Charles Darwin.

Thomas's story is a sad one. Travelling alone, he was admitted under Warrant to our Asylum just over three months ago and, though slightly malnourished, presented as physically well. In conversation, however, he was deluded on the most peculiar of matters, all confined in some way to eating utensils. Though now more settled, his odd beliefs persist. Yet he has worked well in the gardens, and the attendants have come to respect his courteous and eloquent presence with us.

One week ago, Thomas's breathing became more rapid. Now febrile, he refuses almost all nourishment and barely rises from his bed. Although in obvious discomfort, he speaks only of forks and knives and spoons. We have tried analgesics and sedatives — I fear prayer is next.

If your schedule allows, I would be grateful if you would examine Thomas while in London. One opportunity may be the following — at the conclusion of Buller's lecture, we will depart en masse to the Asylum for lunch. Afterwards, I have asked Sippi to lead the members on a tour of the grounds and, if time allows, an inspection of one or two wards. We might then part from the group in order to assess Thomas. He is now in one of the Cottages, and we could rejoin the meeting once the afternoon session begins. Your diagnostic opinion and treatment recommendations would be thankfully received — no doubt by the Darwin family as well.

In closing, please apprise us of any needed assistance with respect to lodging. A reminder — reduced railway fares are available to members of the Dominion Medical Association. Finally, I would be remiss if I did not indicate my profound respect for your work and its influence on my recent publication, which I have sent by separate post. We are truly fortunate to have your expertise in our midst!

Yours most sincerely,

Richard M. Bucke
Medical Superintendent
London Asylum

PART ONE

THOMAS DARWIN

ONE

DOWN HOUSE

Thomas Darwin was born on December 10th, 1857, the eleventh and last child of Charles Robert Darwin and his wife Emma (née Wedgwood). All but three of the Darwin children reached the age of majority. Mary Eleanor, third born, died in infancy in 1842 while the much-loved Annie succumbed in her tenth year in 1851. Charles Waring, born developmentally disabled one year earlier than Thomas, died at only two years of age in 1858. Of Thomas's seven surviving siblings (William Erasmus, Henrietta Emma, George Howard, Elizabeth, Francis, Leonard, and Horace), Horace was the closest in age to Thomas, but almost seven years his senior. As a result of his much younger age, Thomas grew up in relative isolation from his older brothers and sisters, particularly during his adolescent years.

Home was Down House, a large residence sixteen miles south of London, England, located on the outskirts of the small village of Down (now spelled Downe) in the county of Kent. Charles and Emma Darwin moved to this quiet countryside some three

Figure 1. Down House

years after their marriage, having found the social commitments of London society poorly suited to Charles's health. After settling in Down House in 1841, and with the considerable aid of a large domestic staff, they resided there with contentment throughout their forty years of married life.

Oddly, the earliest accounts concerning Thomas's infancy and toddler years are found within the scientific literature. Charles Darwin was a loving and attentive father, but a child's arrival was also an opportunity for the close scrutiny of a domesticated species of interest. Charles studied Thomas intensely, as he had his other children, and the initial observations of his youngest son were recorded in a vellum-bound diary, still extant as *Appendix IV* of the *Oxbridge Unabridged Correspondence of Charles Darwin*.

The notes begin with a meticulous account of Thomas's reflex actions. Thomas first yawned on the third day of his life. On day thirteen, he sneezed. Between three and four weeks of age, he began to startle at loud noises. As Thomas slowly matured, his father's brief comments evolved into more complex observations. By carefully monitoring Thomas's facial expressions and the circumstances in which they occurred, Charles effectively recorded Thomas's earliest experiences of anger, fear, affection, pleasure, shyness, and even his sense of morality.

It was at four months of age that Thomas first expressed fear. Until then, Charles had delighted

Thomas by playing peek-a-boo while galloping on an oversized rocking horse, a family heirloom. On the evening of April 10th, 1858, however, Charles and the horse unexpectedly toppled quite violently. Thomas's moment of surprise quickly transformed into stupefied amazement and then fear. Charles, lying prostrate and injured, still managed to note that, as Thomas watched, powerless, from his crib, his son's eyebrows were raised and both his eyes and mouth were widely opened. In recounting the melodrama, Charles acknowledged he had reflexively scanned the rocking horse for signs of terror, searching specifically for dilated nostrils. Subsequently, Thomas would whimper whenever his father tried to reinitiate the game and the rocking horse was soon removed from the nursery.

Thomas's calm demeanour was rarely broken and Charles recorded only one ill-tempered outburst. At seven months of age, Thomas glared fiercely when his nurse inadvertently dropped the bottle from which he was feeding. Gums clenched, Thomas briefly raised his hands as if to strike the offending nurse, but quickly reverted to passivity. The first indication of Thomas's sense of injustice and morality soon followed. At eight months of age, Thomas refused to kiss an older sister, possibly Henrietta, when she declined to share her last piece of liquorice.

A notable feature of the entire diary (which ended when Thomas was eighteen months of age) is the frequent comparisons found within its entries. On the more pedestrian level, the timings of Thomas's developmental milestones were consistently cross-referenced to those of his brothers and sisters. In general, Thomas's progression was roughly equivalent to that of his siblings. Thomas did, however, show a much earlier aptitude for drawing, a fine motor skill he acquired when only fifteen months of age.

The far more interesting correlations were Charles Darwin's whimsical comparisons of Thomas's development to a diverse range of plants and animals. Insectivorous plants were more excitable, iguanas more agile, and rhododendron seeds much hardier. The most unusual inference was when Thomas's melodious intonation of "Oh, Oh!" was deemed analogous to the musical utterances of the short-beaked tumbler pigeon.

Throughout Thomas's infancy, Charles also subjected his youngest son to an ongoing series of experiments that were conducted with the assistance of the other Darwin children. To test Thomas's startle response, Charles recruited Francis to play his bassoon from variable distances and directions. To test Thomas's reflex withdrawal, Elizabeth was instructed to stimulate specific areas of Thomas's limbs and torso with strips of blotting paper. Thomas tolerated the attention with good humour.

Always inquisitive, Charles's conjectures and theories eventually became too much for Emma.

Shortly after Thomas had begun breastfeeding, Charles noted that Thomas would protrude his lips whenever Emma's bosom approached within five to six inches. After excluding any correlation with vision or touch, Charles generated a list of alternative explanations that included a possible association to the position in which Thomas was cradled when about to be fed. Although Thomas seemed unfazed, Emma could not bear the delay in feeding occasioned by Charles's constant requests for Emma to withdraw her breast, reposition Thomas in her arms, and to again thrust her by then oozing breast towards Thomas. An exasperated Emma requested Charles to refrain from attending further breastfeeding sessions, a maternal injunction he amenably recorded and obeyed.

Though not intended as such, Charles's notes concerning Thomas amount to an engaging biographical sketch of an infant, publishable immediately as an independent manuscript had Charles wished to do so. Instead, he characteristically delayed publication and chose to include selected observations of Thomas in a much later work titled *The Expression of the Emotions in Man and Animals*, printed in 1872. Here, Charles's meticulous surveillance of Thomas and the other Darwin children aided his delineation of thirty-four distinct emotional states in man. A careful reading of *Expression of the Emotions* reveals that depictions made under the headings of

Figure 2. Photographs Used to Depict Suffering and
Weeping. In Darwin, C. *The Expression of the
Emotions in Man and Animals*. London:
John Murray, 1872.

"Meditation," "Self-Attention," and "Shyness" pertained to Thomas. Though circumscribed in nature, Thomas's three appearances within *Expression of the Emotions* convey a thoughtful and sensitive child.

The evocation of "Shyness" is particularly poignant. After a week's absence to obtain treatment at Dr. Lane's hydropathic establishment,[3] Charles was touched by Thomas's response on his return home. Just seventeen months of age, Thomas initially averted his eyes and attempted to hide his face in his mother's dress as Charles warmly greeted Emma and his other children. After hesitating briefly, Thomas then reached out to hug his elated father.

Other early glimpses of Thomas can be found within his mother's correspondence. When younger, Emma frequently exchanged letters with many of her Darwin and Wedgwood relatives, particularly her Aunt Fanny Allen. At first, Emma enjoyed describing the activities of her children, especially William, Annie, and Henrietta. By the time Thomas was born, however, Emma's writing had begun to take on a reserved and less personal quality. Emma's earliest mention of Thomas occurred in association with his first birthday.

---

3. In mid-nineteenth century England, hydropathic treatment (or the water cure) for nervous disorders was a fashionable prescription for the upper classes. Charles Darwin employed it with uneven results, at various establishments, between 1849 and 1863.

Down, Friday Dec 10th [1858]

My dearest Aunt Fanny,

It was so pleasant to receive your affectionate letter on this special date. Our dear Thomas is one year old today. His brothers and sisters adore him; he is so delicate and quiet. Yet still I am tired and drained. How thankful I will be when the children no longer require such constant care and attention. Even then I suppose Charles will never want to be alone. My poor Charles. His stomach aches again and he has been very uncomfortable.

Yours, E. D.

The letter would prove typical of much of Emma's subsequent correspondence in which Thomas's brief appearances were quickly eclipsed by details of Emma's fatigue or the ill health of Charles or another child. At other times, Emma failed to mention any of her children altogether and instead addressed such details as household accounts, recent visitors, or the latest novel she had read. One exception was a letter Emma wrote many years later to her granddaughter Gwen (née Darwin) Raverat.[4] After

4. Gwen was the oldest child of Thomas's brother George and his wife Maud Du Puy.

thanking Gwen for a recent visit, Emma discloses that Gwen's stay evoked memories of her own children when they were young and the unusual games they would play. She then recounts in detail one amusement that was invented by Henrietta. It required hunting the stinkhorn toadstool exclusively by scent. Emma describes a young blindfolded Thomas as exceptionally adept at sniffing his way around the unmown meadow behind Down House until, "with a sudden leap," he fell upon his "pungent" prey. The only other mention of Thomas within the letter is a brief reference to his death: "Tragically, your Uncle Thomas died of tuberculosis while travelling in Canada at age twenty-one."

In confiding in Gwen Raverat, Emma may have been responding to her granddaughter's interest in hearing such family anecdotes. Although Gwen never met her Uncle Thomas (she was born in 1885), she later wrote *Period Piece: A Cambridge Childhood*, an extended family memoir that places Thomas's childhood (and health) in a helpful context. According to Gwen, all but one of Thomas's siblings suffered from nervous difficulties. Elizabeth was "very stout and nervous," Henrietta had "been an invalid all her life" and was portrayed as having an insane fear of germs; Francis seemed to have "no spring of hope in him," Leonard "inherited the family hypochondria in a mild degree," Horace "always retained traces of the invalid's outlook," while

Gwen's father, George, had "nerves always as taut as fiddle strings."

Henrietta was the most disturbed: "When there were colds about she often wore a kind of gas-mask of her own invention. It was an ordinary wire kitchen-strainer, stuffed with antiseptic cotton-wool, and tied on like a snout, with elastic over her ears. In this she would receive her visitors and discuss politics in a hollow voice out of her eucalyptus-scented seclusion, oblivious of the fact that they might be struggling with fits of laughter."

In accounting for his children's astonishingly poor health, Charles Darwin blamed himself. He was certain they had inherited what he viewed as his constitutional weakness: various and often ill-defined symptoms that began shortly after his travels aboard the *Beagle* as a young man. Charles's most consistent and distressing complaint was gastric discomfort associated with retching, chiefly at night. If severe, his stomach pains were accompanied by alarming, hysterical fits of crying. Charles also experienced uncomfortable cardiac palpitations as well as eczematous skin eruptions. At times he was incapacitated, enduring at least three episodes of prolonged sickness.

Charles's diverse ailments were a constant worry to his family and he, in turn, fretted incessantly over the health of his children. He became particularly anxious following the death of his son Charles Waring, who had been born one year prior to Thomas and died June 28th, 1858, during a scarlet fever epidemic. Deeply affected by the loss, Charles became panic-stricken that Thomas would also fall ill. For the remainder of that year, an exhausted Charles monitored Thomas's breathing during the night. When finally challenged by Emma, Charles cited the nocturnal habits of the Indian Telegraph plant, explaining that circadian rhythms could significantly stress breathing patterns. Emma was unconvinced and forbade Charles from further disturbing both his and Thomas's sleep.

Despite his ill health, Charles Darwin maintained a relentless and rigid work schedule. Each day, as a rule, he was in his study, quietly reading, writing, and attending to correspondence, or carefully dissecting the latest specimen to arrive by post. While Charles professed to require absolute solitude while working and wished to be interrupted only in urgent circumstances, he in fact welcomed his children's playful intrusions. Thomas would peek in and, with his father's assent, tiptoe quietly across the study to read silently by the fireplace. Charles would often take such opportune moments to instruct Thomas on the use of various scientific instruments. At age eight, Thomas was reported by Emma to have looked up from his father's dissecting microscope and said, "Do you think, Papa, that I shall be this happy all my future life?"

Throughout his childhood, Thomas also joined his father on the Sandwalk, a "thinking path" Charles had built behind Down House. Thomas and Charles enjoyed the constitutionals they shared round its circuitous course, which was named for the sand used to dress its surface. One summer, Charles grew curious about the bees that disturbed their otherwise contemplative walks. In the guise of a game, he recruited Thomas and his brothers to track the bees' movements. After dispersing his sons around the Sandwalk, Charles instructed each to yell out "Bee!" as one flew by. Charles would reposition his assistants in accordance with these cries and, in time, the bees' regular lines of flight were determined. Thomas was adroit at sightings and would fearlessly tear after the bees as they flew by. An agitated Charles, fearing Thomas might be stung, would quickly redirect his youngest son back to his original post.

Even with Charles's persistent anxiety over Thomas's health, the two enjoyed an affectionate relationship. It was Emma, however, who attended more directly to Thomas's day-to-day needs. She was forty-nine when Thomas was born (Charles was forty-eight). Undeterred by the risks associated with pregnancy at her advanced age, and often restricted to bed rest due to her pronounced morning sickness and fatigue, Emma tolerated her confinement with Thomas without complaint. Thomas's earlier than anticipated birth was precipitous. Finding his wife suddenly in labour, and with Henrietta and Elizabeth at his side, an apprehensive Charles had administered chloroform as they waited for the local doctor to arrive. An over-sedated Emma was virtually unconscious when Thomas was delivered.

In between doting on Charles, raising her other children, and supervising a large household staff, Emma cared for Thomas in her characteristically pragmatic fashion. Resurrecting storybooks she had written years before as a young Sunday school teacher, Emma also served as Thomas's first tutor. It was from such simple Bible stories that Thomas was taught both reading and religion — what Charles fondly referred to as his wife's abridged version of the three Rs. Thomas's religious instruction was of central importance to Emma. Even as a toddler, it was compulsory that a scrubbed and well-dressed Thomas walk with Emma, and all those siblings then at home, to the local church. After services, Emma would exchange pleasantries with the other families in the small adjoining churchyard. Although Emma encouraged Thomas to play with the other children, he preferred to linger at her side, "Alone, but not lonely," according to Emma.

Thomas also participated from an early age in his mother's charitable affairs. Revered by the parish community, Emma quietly supported those who were ill or in financial need. Each week, with Thomas as her "assistant," she prepared homemade remedies that were then dispensed to grateful congregants, often with an accompanying food basket. Many of her medicinal recipes were based on prescriptions first written by Thomas's physician grandfather, Dr. Robert Waring Darwin. Although all her generous parcels were appreciated, a particular favourite with the parishioners was Emma's potent gin cordial laced with opium.

Thomas proved helpful in the kitchen, at first retrieving the various ingredients from the "physic cupboard" that Emma would carefully weigh and measure. As he grew older, he took direction from both Emma and Mrs. Evans, the family cook who served the Darwins for many years. One of Thomas's early chores was to assist Mrs. Evans in the scullery, a small room beside the kitchen where the dishes and kitchen utensils were scrubbed. Despite difficulty in reaching the top-most drawers, Thomas's responsibilities soon included returning the cleaned cutlery and serving pieces to the large antique sideboard that ran the length of the Darwin dining room.

In addition to their impressive Wedgwood dinner service,[5] the Darwins also owned a large and eclectic assortment of serving utensils, as Emma often entertained her extended family. A number of these implements, such as marrow forks and cream ladles, were curious in appearance and Mrs. Evans

5. Now referred to as the Darwin Water Lily pattern.

would challenge Thomas to identify their purpose as the two worked together. Though only four years old, Thomas immediately recognized that a u-shaped, narrow-bladed set of tongs was used to serve asparagus. Not even his father had initially appreciated their function. Many years before, the piece had been mailed to Charles as a wedding gift from his friend J. M. Herbert. In the accompanying letter, Herbert, in an effort to be amusing, only drolly stated the enclosed gift was a representative of the genus *Forficula* (a reference to the common earwig, an insect that the silver utensil apparently resembled). To reward Thomas's unexpected acumen, Mrs. Evans insisted thereafter on serving him the first portion of roasted asparagus whenever she prepared the seasonal vegetable. Though Thomas disliked asparagus and would have far preferred priority for Mrs. Evans's gingerbread, he graciously accepted the asparagus as the gift he knew it to be.

On turning five, Thomas began to receive sporadic tutoring from Mr. Brodie Innes, vicar of Down. Mr. Innes focussed on expanding Thomas's reading and writing skills, and also introduced Thomas to basic arithmetic. Though Thomas learned to add and subtract, Mr. Innes had little talent for teaching. Recognizing his own limitations, he encouraged Emma to allow Thomas to join his sisters Henrietta (while she was still at home) and Elizabeth in the small schoolroom at Down House, where a series of daily governesses supervised the girls' home schooling. As Emma Darwin held strongly that the "Devil finds work for idle hands," the emphasis of the girls' education was skewed towards embroidery and handicrafts. As one activity, Thomas made a number of flimsy Easter baskets. He had intended to present individual members of his family with an identical holiday gift but each basket was significantly and disappointingly distinct from its predecessor. Thomas would later conclude that such imperfect production was an important source of diversity in the world of artefacts.

Thomas also attended his sisters' weekly Wednesday Drawing Class in the local village. Miss Mary Matheson, the teacher, was a diffident but well-intentioned spinster whose style of instruction was to emphasize accuracy over artistic interpretation. Although never hesitant to erase errant lines, she was genuinely supportive, and Thomas was a conscientious pupil. While Thomas was self-deprecating about his ability to draw, these early lessons came to useful advantage. He later produced his own illustrations for the manuscripts he authored.

If the weather was remotely tolerable, Thomas was excused from all lessons and allowed to play outside. Emma and Charles were permissive parents, and their sole stipulation was that Thomas remain in earshot of the one o'clock bell for lunch, the family's principal meal of the day. Thomas would spend hours digging in the sandy soil of the kitchen garden and the orchard, deploying toy soldiers on the ample lawn, and inspecting the considerable number of birds' nests in the trees that bordered the Sandwalk. A favourite sanctuary was a small abandoned summer house, just beyond the Sandwalk, where Thomas enjoyed drawing in chalk on its decaying wooden walls.

The only drawback to such activities was their solitary nature. For most of Thomas's childhood, his brothers were either at boarding school or living away from home. On occasion, Parslow, the Darwins' long-serving butler, would challenge Thomas to a game of quoits. Akin to horseshoes, this entailed tossing rings towards a spike in the ground some distance away. To Parslow's irritation, Thomas's throws were rarely accurate and he was prone to closing his eyes and simply hurling the rings as far as he could. This resulted in long, and at times fruitless, searches for the hard-to-find rings.

When available, Thomas's favourite outdoor play-fellow was his father, but Charles seldom had the energy to engage in child-driven games. For more consistent fellowship, Thomas relied on the cows, pigs, and ducks that also resided on the eighteen acres upon which Down House stood. During Charles's "pigeon phase," Thomas spent considerable time in his father's pigeon house, where he quickly learned to mimic a number of pigeon sounds, including their warning call of distress: *coo roo-c'too-coo*. Thereafter, and with the amused collusion of his father, Thomas would loudly sound *coo roo-c'too-coo* each time a member of the clergy called upon the Darwins. A forewarned Charles could then hurriedly retreat to his bedroom with an apparent exacerbation of any number of physical symptoms, much to Emma's annoyance.

Thomas was also inclined to flee to his bedroom to avoid company and was generally perceived as shy. His smallish room was located on the second floor, one of the many bedrooms in Down House's large three-storey structure, which had been altered and expanded over the years to accommodate the growing numbers of Darwins and domestic staff. One means to entice Thomas downstairs was the sound of a billiards game. Just prior to Thomas's birth, a billiards table had been installed in the old dining room, and the game immediately became a favourite form of recreation for the entire household. It was Thomas's task to methodically organize the balls at the beginning of each family tournament using a triangular rack that had been crafted expertly out of cork by Jackson, the Darwins' groom.[6] Charles often

---

6. Jackson succeeded Parslow as the Darwins' butler in 1875. Jackson's great passion had been the building of a scale model of Down House made entirely from pieces of cork. Despite some initial reluctance by the curator, this unique model now resides in a small museum within Down House.

won, likely because Emma had instructed her sons "never to beat Papa."

Thomas would also leave the security of his room on the sound of a secret knock. Thomas's bedroom was directly beside larger quarters shared by Henrietta and Elizabeth. On hearing three taps in rapid succession, Thomas would dutifully open his door and descend partway down the staircase as his sisters furtively dressed in their mother's jewels and wardrobe. The former were kept in a simple locked wooden box that first had to be quietly removed from their mother's room. As the key fitted badly, Henrietta and Emma often resorted to violently shaking and bashing the box before it would open. Again, Thomas's skills as a pigeon were required as he timed loud calls of *coo roo-c'too-coo* to mask the sounds arising from his sisters' inept thievery. These calls had the unintended consequence of also sending his well-trained father scurrying to his room only to emerge some time later, uncertain as to whether any of his physical symptoms were still required. Otherwise, when not involved in such clandestine activities, Thomas preferred to spend long hours in his comfortable but cluttered room, reading, drawing, and, most satisfying of all, organizing his various collections.

From a young age, Thomas was an entrenched collector. Though he amassed all sorts of objects, his greatest passion was for accumulating buttons.

These were organized by size, shape, and colour, and were sorted into trays and jars that Thomas appropriated from his father's dissecting supplies. As Thomas's expertise increased, he also began to identify each button on the basis of its composition. This was challenging, as many button materials closely resembled each other. Thomas taught himself to insert a fine, heated needle in the back of each button in order to smell for a distinct odour, such as the stagnant saltwater smell associated with tortoiseshell. The technique was time-consuming, but it allowed Thomas to sort and re-sort his buttons according to finer distinctions and also garnered his father's admiration for his methodical perseverance.

Although Thomas was free to retire to his room as he wished, he was generally expected to spend evenings with other members of his family. After a relatively late and simple tea, it was the Darwins' custom to gather in their large unpretentious drawing-room. This was a time for discussion, affable loitering, and two rituals, the first of which was the collective reading aloud of novels.[7] Thomas's

---

7. A notable aspect of these readings was the editorial transgressions. One infamous desecration involved Elizabeth's abridged rendition of *Henry IV*, in which she refused to read a single line uttered by Falstaff. According to Elizabeth, "*Henry IV* would be such a good play without Falstaff." *Down: The Home of the Darwins,* Atkins H. (London: Royal College of Surgeons of England, 1974) p.55.

favourite story was *The Ugly Duckling* as read by Henrietta. His eldest sister was masterful at impersonating the ducks whose dialogue animated the fairy tale. At one point in the story, a mother duck instructs her ducklings to "now bow your necks, and say 'quack.'" Taking his cue, Thomas would dutifully bend his neck and boisterously "quack" along with Henrietta, much to the pleasure of the Darwin household.

Charles's enjoyment of Thomas's participation was twofold. Aside from revelling in Thomas's joie de vivre, the transformation of a homely and unwanted baby bird into a graceful and beautiful swan was for Charles, above all, a "eugenics" parable.[8] Although a swan's egg had accidentally rolled into a duck's nest, the ultimate superiority of the "ugly duckling" over the other barnyard ducks was predetermined by its genetic lineage. Charles, who supported the concept of selective breeding, saw Thomas's enthusiasm for *The Ugly Ducking* as a sign he was a fellow eugenicist, one who recognized the importance of nature over nurture.

After the shared pleasure of reading, it was then time for backgammon, the second of the evening rit-

---

8. A particularly strong proponent for the eugenics movement was Charles's half-cousin Francis Galton. Galton advocated for increased breeding of genetically superior "gifted individuals." Although Charles was sympathetic to his cousin's proposal, he viewed it as a utopian fantasy.

uals. The games played by Charles and Emma were undertaken seriously, with Charles uncharacteristically boasting on one occasion, "Now the tally with my wife in backgammon stands thus: she, poor creature, has won only 2490 games, whilst I have won, hurrah, hurrah, 2795 games!" Although the children were expected to remain neutral, Thomas and his siblings would openly cheer their mother's victories.

Following backgammon, Emma, a competent pianist, might then entertain the family by playing a number of classical pieces. This was an opportunity for Thomas to do his schoolwork, to read, or to quietly withdraw to his room. By half past ten, it was bedtime for Thomas and the entire Darwin household.

TWO

SCHOOL DAYS

At age ten, following the summer of 1868, Thomas was enrolled at Clapham, the school where each of his brothers (except William) had been educated. He remained there as a boarding student until the age of nineteen. As in other private boarding schools in Victorian England, lessons were confined predominantly to the study of classics. Instructional methods emphasized rote learning and verse-making. For most students, the tedium was only partially relieved by compulsory participation in the seasonal athletic programs (usually cricket, football, cross-country running, and fencing), the appalling and repetitive school meals, and time spent, after last bell, avoiding the abuses of senior boys.

Each student's stay at Clapham was associated with an individual casebook (or student file). Under the date September 14th, 1868, Thomas's name stands in the General Admission Register: "Thomas Darwin, son of Charles Darwin, of Down" along with the modest, albeit misleading, description of his father's occupation — "country gentleman." Within his student file, still housed along with those of his classmates in the National Archives of England, cursory identifying data is followed by the headmaster's brief yearly note, each dated on or around June 1st, from 1869 to 1877 inclusive.

The annual notes for each student were virtually identical, and those written in the first few years of Thomas's enrollment by a Mr. Pritchard are hardly illuminating.

> "June 1st, 1869. Thomas has passed the year's examinations and is eligible for advancement. Pritchard."
> "June 1st, 1870. Ibid."
> "June 1st, 1871. Ibid."

In autumn, 1871, a Dr. Wrigley was appointed the new headmaster and, perhaps due to a newcomer's enthusiasm, a more substantial note next appeared in Thomas's casebook.

> "June 3rd, 1872. Thomas is a quiet and obedient boy of avrage [*sic*] ability. Isolated but cooperative when approached. Hardworking, honest, and upright. Eligible for advancement. Wrigley."

Wrigley's assessment confirmed Charles and Emma's fears. Although doubtlessly pleased with Dr. Wrigley's positive estimation of Thomas's character, the two had privately hoped that, once enrolled at Clapham, Thomas might engage in the typical male camaraderie of adolescence. Until then, they had attributed Thomas's solitary nature to a lack of social opportunity. To Charles and Emma's disappointment, however, Thomas remained uninterested in acquiring close friends even when surrounded by boys his age. "Still alone but not lonely," as a resigned Emma reported to Aunt Fanny.

After his initial note, Wrigley's annual entries succumbed to the formulaic. Thomas continued to be promoted annually, and in his final year at Clapham, he capably passed the entrance examinations for Cambridge. Charles and Emma seemed content with Thomas's consistent, if unremarkable, school performance. Based on Emma's correspondence, Thomas's single frustration was his inability to find like-minded hobbyists. "The children are well ... As for Thomas, he is still at Clapham. He seems to have inherited a dislike of Greek and Latin, but otherwise attends to his work seriously. Charles and I were not surprised that his efforts to start a Button Club failed to attract a single fellow. Yet overall, he has been quite contented there."[9]

Although Clapham was a boarding school, it

9. This was the last letter Emma would write to her favourite aunt. On May 6th, 1875, Miss Fanny Allen died in her ninety-fourth year. Emma's daughter Elizabeth eventually compiled and edited Fanny and Emma's correspondence, published

was located just six miles from Down House and, due to this proximity, Thomas routinely returned home for weekends during school terms, as well as for summer recesses. By now he was also viewed as sufficiently mature to assist his father's research. Although overshadowed in significance by his "species" work, Charles Darwin was then conducting a series of botanical experiments, often with the aid not only of his gardener and under-gardener, but of his family as well. Their laboratory, initially the extensive garden at Down House, was later supplemented by the addition of a small hothouse.

Throughout the early 1870s, Thomas played an essential role in confirming his father's discovery that the plant *Drosera* (more commonly known as the sundew) was capable of trapping and, seemingly, digesting insects. Charles had noticed the sundew, "when properly excited", secreted a substance analogous to an animal's digestive fluid. In the experiments required to substantiate this observation, it was Thomas's task to "excite" the plants. At first, Thomas chose to leave raw meat on the sundew's sticky glandular tentacles. By chance, Thomas then discovered that emotional encouragement enhanced the sun-

in 1920 as *My Dearest Aunt Fanny, My Dear Emma: The Correspondence of Mrs. Emma (Wedgwood) Darwin and Miss Fanny Allen*. Elizabeth subsequently published an additional volume of her mother's correspondence titled *Dear Emma*, an exhaustive exchange of Emma's letters to and from her nieces, nephews, and grandchildren.

dew's secretions. His technique progressed from rather crude facial distortions to more effective gentle caresses of the plant's uppermost stem, sometimes cooing as he did so. His father's book, *Insectivorous Plants*, in which Charles acknowledged Thomas's contribution, was published in 1875. Thomas subsequently assisted with the experiments his father conducted on the formation of vegetable mould as well as those related to the fertilization and movements of various plants.[10]

When time allowed, Thomas continued to enlarge his button collection. To his regret, one ill-advised acquisition led to a rare fraternal altercation. After removing a great horn button from his brother Leonard's new jacket, and substituting a small, glued piece of cardboard, Thomas was angrily confronted by the usually even-tempered Leonard. Thomas immediately apologized and reattached the original horn button using stiff copper wire. "As good as new!" according to Emma. Nevertheless, Leonard now mistrusted Thomas and, for the next few months, insisted on hiding all his clothes under an old chesterfield in the drawing-room.

It was during this period of tension that Thomas turned to coin collecting, a new interest sparked by

10. In his book, *The Formation of Vegetable Mould, through the Action of Worms, with Observations on their Habits* (1881), Charles Darwin concluded that the formation of vegetable mould was due to the digestive process of the common earthworm.

a welcome discovery. Sometime in early 1869, when out for a hike with Horace, Thomas came across what he believed were two ancient British coins. Encouraged by their father, the two brothers reported the find, published on February 25th, 1869, in the *London Numismatics Monthly Intelligencer*. Accompanying the submission was Thomas's confident pencil sketch of the two coins.

COINAGE OF THE ANCIENT BRITONS AT DOWN

> We wish to report that one of us (T. D.) has recently found on Keston Common in the parish of Down, six miles from the village of Bromley, two very old coins, which we believe to be of ancient British origin. One, which appears the older, depicts the image of a head on its obverse; on the reverse there are a chariot and four horses (Fig. A). The depictions on the second coin are much less detailed. On the obverse there is now only a laurel wreath; a single horse on the reverse (Fig. B). As Keston Common is so close to London, we have thought that you might like to include this little notice in the *Intelligencer*.
>
> Horace Darwin and Thomas Darwin, Down, Kent

FIG. A

FIG. B

Figure 3. Two Ancient British Coins
(Illustrations by Thomas Darwin, from
"Coinage of the Ancient Britons at Down," 1869).

The published report indicated the coins were found in Keston Common, a lowland heath located about two miles from Down House. This setting was to take on a more ominous connotation for Thomas just a few months later. Some years before, his father had been prescribed horseback riding for therapeutic purposes and had found the grasslands and fields of the nearby common a convenient place to ride. Although his ill health persisted, Charles enjoyed the exercise until one day in early April, 1869, when his "quiet cob Tommy stumbled and fell, rolling on him and bruising him seriously." Thomas witnessed the misadventure and was traumatized. Shaken, he retreated into his bedroom for a number of days, consoling himself with repeated games of shadow puppets. Thereafter, he had an aversion to horses and experienced significant anxiety in their presence. Although Charles Darwin never raised the matter with either Emma or Thomas, he was privately convinced the earlier rocking horse incident was responsible for his son's brief, but otherwise puzzling, regression.

When not working or in school, Thomas's adolescence was also characterized by the social milestones and activities of a large Victorian family. The happier occasions included the marriages of three siblings: Henrietta Emma to Richard Buckley Litchfield in 1871; Francis to Amy Richenda Ruck in 1874; and William Erasmus to Sara Sedgwick in 1877.

In 1876, the birth of Thomas's first nephew

Figure 4. Charles Darwin on His Horse Tommy

(Bernard) was followed by the tragic loss of Bernard's young mother who, just one week later, died of puerperal fever. Afterwards, Thomas's widowed brother Francis returned to Down House with his young son. Although the baby was a great joy to the entire household, Bernard had a particular affinity for Thomas, an affection that was shared. Together, they would search for gooseberries in the woods surrounding Down House so that Grandmamma Emma could make her much-loved gooseberry cream. Thomas would also spend long hours gently pushing Bernard on the swing that Thomas's Uncle Erasmus (known as Uncle Ras) had suspended between two yew trees years before.

One favourite family anecdote concerning Thomas and Bernard involved a secret potion. Charles had once taken pleasure in astounding a very young Thomas with variously dyed polyanthuses and primroses that he produced by watering the plants with coloured fluids. It became Uncle Thomas's responsibility to educate his nephew in similar manner. A triumphant Bernard was then allowed to present these alchemic concoctions to his father Francis and to Grandmamma and Grandpapa. Even Charles Darwin feigned amazement and would beg to learn from a pleased and proud Bernard how such transformations had been achieved.

Thomas and Bernard's mutual joy was Polly, a rough white terrier and cherished Darwin family pet. Generally docile and content to remain indoors,

Polly would sit serenely for hours, staring out the drawing-room window. On sighting Thomas and Bernard in the gardens, however, she would madly bark and race around the drawing-room, mollified only on reuniting with her glimpsed masters. Such enthusiasm was deemed worthy of description by Charles Darwin, and Polly's contortions are reported in much greater detail under the heading of "Exuberance" in the second edition of *Expression of the Emotions*, published posthumously in 1890.[11]

Throughout Thomas's youth, the Darwins occasionally undertook brief family holidays, in Emma's hope that a change of scenery would improve her husband's frail health. Journeys of note involving Thomas included a trip to Torquay in June and July of 1861; a house in Malvern Wells in the autumn of 1863; six weeks in Dimbola Lodge, Isle of Wight, during the summer of 1868; and time spent in Caerdeon, in

---

11. Polly also played a role in Charles Darwin's observation that certain characteristics in an offspring could revert to those of an ancestor. As Francis Darwin recounted, "She had a mark on her back where she had been burnt, and where the hair had re-grown red instead of white, and my father used to commend her for this tuft of hair as being in accordance with his theory of pangenesis; her father had been a red bull-terrier, thus the red hair appearing after the burn showed the presence of latent red gemmules." Polly died two days after Charles Darwin's death and was buried in the front yard at Down House. (Darwin, C. *The Autobiography of Charles Darwin, and Selected Letters*. New York: Dover Publications, 1958. p.74.)

North Wales, in the summer of 1869. In 1872, Thomas travelled independently to Staffordshire where he summered with his Wedgwood relations. There, he worked during the day at the Etruria Works Pottery, founded by his maternal great-grandfather Josiah Wedgwood I. It was then common for boys his age to carry moulds from the potters to the stoves — tedious and dangerous employment. Other risks also had to be considered. Emma, for one, was extremely concerned that Thomas, only fifteen, might be prematurely attracted to one of many first cousins he met during this visit. By her count, there were already four first cousin marriages involving the Darwin and Wedgwood families, including Emma's own marriage to Charles. As Emma confided to her Aunt Fanny Allen, "There is such a strong inclination on both sides of Thomas's family to marry first cousins."

Emma suspected that Thomas's affections would be most vulnerable while attending the large family dances held at Maer Hall, the Wedgwood's country home. Thankfully, at least from Emma's perspective, Thomas had once attended a dancing class with his sisters Henrietta and Elizabeth. Just seven, and the only boy, Thomas had been forced to wear baggy velvet knickerbockers that ended above his knees. After class, Emma found him sobbing outside on the curbstone. The unpleasant association remained with Thomas and it was a relieved Emma who wrote to Aunt Fanny that, "Thomas, having never taken to

Figure 5. Etruria Works

dancing, has resisted all overtures to join his cousins on the dance floor. Hurrah, hurrah!"

Charles was also worried that Thomas might be captivated by a first cousin, but not because Thomas was too young. Based on his readings and his botanical experiments, Charles had become aware that inbred plants frequently perished or otherwise fared poorly when forced to compete with other plants. Fearing that the ill effects of inbreeding also applied to other species, and that his and Emma's children were thereby at-risk, Charles lobbied to have the Census Act of 1871 address the prevalence of cousin marriages. After this effort proved unsuccessful, Charles then encouraged his son George to statistically examine whether concerns about cousin marriages were justified.[12] To assist his research, George conscripted Thomas's services for the entire summer of 1873.

It became Thomas's task to identify all same-surname marriages announced in the *Pall Mall Gazette* (between the years 1869 and 1872) and as they appeared in the pedigrees of *Burke's Landed Gentry*. There were a number of confounding variables, as not all same-surname marriages reflected marriage between cousins, and different-name first cousin marriages were not identified. Nevertheless,

12. George was later appointed to the Plumian Chair of Astronomy and Experimental Philosophy and had a distinguished scientific career, which included knighthood. The evolution of the solar system was one of his academic interests.

Thomas's meticulous gleanings allowed his brother to cautiously estimate the proportion of cousin marriages in the general population. George then examined data addressing the death rate amongst the offspring of cousins as well as whether first cousin marriages had any effect on the production of insanity or idiocy. Although he felt the prevailing concerns regarding first cousin marriages were exaggerated, George regrettably concluded that he, Thomas, and all others in similar hereditary circumstances were indeed at greater risk for various ill-defined maladies.

Whether the above analyses dissuaded or redirected Thomas's amorous inclinations, if any, is unclear. As Thomas grew older, however, the nature of Emma's concern shifted. She began to wish Thomas would show more interest in the daughters of various acquaintances, worrying that Thomas might ultimately choose the "companionship of clever men at clubs over female chit-chat in the drawing-room."

In summary, Thomas Darwin's adolescence appears to have been relatively benign. School was tolerable, and Down House was, in general, a quiet but easeful residence, punctuated with moments of activity stemming from the comings and goings of his older siblings, the stays of Aunt Fanny or other congenial relations, and the occasional visits of his father's scientific friends. At age nineteen, with the monotony of Clapham successfully behind him, an apparently healthy Thomas left home for Cambridge.

THREE

CAMBRIDGE UNIVERSITY

Thomas Darwin commenced studies at Christ's College, Cambridge University, in the Michaelmas term of 1877.[13] In the previous century, his great-grandfather Erasmus the elder had been the first Darwin to enroll at Cambridge; by the time Thomas arrived for his first term, his father Charles, his Uncle Erasmus, and four of his five older brothers were "Cambridge men."

Despite the strong family tradition, Thomas's choice of Cambridge was not as straightforward as it might seem. Charles Darwin had encouraged Thomas to apply, but he was ambivalent about the worthiness of his alma mater as a place for higher education. Fifty years previously, he had attended Cambridge as a pre-divinity student, graduating a creditable tenth amongst those who were candidates for the ordinary Bachelor of Arts degree. Although

---

13. Then, as today, the academic year at Cambridge was comprised of three terms: Michaelmas: October to December; Lent: January to March; and Easter: April to mid-June. In the year 1877, the Michaelmas term began on October 2nd.

Charles valued his pleasant recollections of friends and outings, he had little regard for the quality of the teaching he received. This frank appraisal almost certainly influenced Thomas's strong preference for self-directed study during his time at Cambridge, despite the range of academic programs that the various colleges of the university offered.

Perhaps Thomas's relatively independent status helps explain why his two years at Cambridge are so sparsely documented. His name is not recorded in the Admission Book at Christ's College, though in those days, it was negligently kept and it was not unusual for new undergraduates to be overlooked. It appears the only existing account by Thomas of his time at Cambridge is a letter he wrote to his father shortly after his arrival (see Chapter 5). Thomas's letter begins, "I am well and now equally well settled — in your old rooms, the Master tells me." In keeping with a tradition at Christ's College, Thomas was assigned the same rooms in which his father resided during his earlier stay at the college (and which his older brother William had also occupied). As a result, Thomas lived in a pleasant panelled set of rooms on the first floor of the front court. Charles Darwin had enjoyed these living quarters immensely and felt they were far preferable to the original lodgings he rented above a Sydney Street tobacconist's shop during his first two Cambridge terms.

Thomas's letter to his father implied he had

Figure 6. Darwin's Old Room at Christ's College

gained membership to the *Plinian Society*.[14] This society was founded in 1823 and consisted of Cambridge undergraduates interested in the natural sciences. Essentially a discussion group, the *Society* provided a milieu for students to read their own scientific papers to one another in an encouraging atmosphere. Thomas took such opportunity on at least three occasions, and two of his oral presentations were published in the *Transactions of the Plinian Society*.

Charles Darwin was delighted that Thomas was attending the *Society* meetings and was able to join him on one celebrated occasion. In 1877, Cambridge had awarded Charles an honorary Doctorate of Law. Despite reservations about the toll this trip might have on his health, he agreed to travel from Down to accept the degree. The ceremony, held at the University's Senate House on November 17th, 1877, was attended by Thomas, Emma, and other members of his family.

The following day, Thomas invited his father to accompany him to that evening's *Plinian Society* meeting. By good fortune, it was one of the alternate Sunday evenings on which the twenty or so

14. The *Plinian Natural History Society* (usually truncated to *Plinian Society*) dissolved in 1888. Transactions of the Society were published quarterly through its later years as were the society's "minute-book" records, in which the agenda and minutes of each meeting were recorded, sometimes in point form.

Plinians met throughout the term. The "minute-book" records of November 18th, 1877 indicate that:

> "At the insistence of the Society, our esteemed guest Mr. Charles Darwin summarized key tenets of his theory of natural selection. Mr. Charles Darwin also discussed his and Thomas's recent studies of the action of worms, and the significant amount of soil they could move. Mr. Charles Darwin shared his theory that it was on account of earthworms that the ancient stones at Stonehenge were slowly settling into the soil and would eventually disappear altogether. At the end of the evening, Mr. Charles Darwin was loudly cheered, and the entire membership volunteered to excavate Stonehenge should Mr. Charles Darwin ever need such assistance."

Charles and Emma's trip was a short one, and they returned the next morning to Down House. Though exhausted by the travel and the obligatory functions, they were delighted to have found Thomas so comfortably settled in his new surroundings. In fact, Thomas was already deeply immersed in his own scientific enquiry. After attending the lectures of Pitt Rivers, an anthropologist who used Australian aboriginal weapons and other artefacts to illustrate his opinions (see Chapter 5), Thomas had suddenly realized that his father's theories could be applied to more than just successive forms of organic life. Thomas now had only one goal — to account for the origin and diversity of artefacts in a manner analogous to his father's evolutionary theories on biological change. In what seem to be more affectionate moments, Thomas referred to the artefacts under his study as "my special world of inanimate objects."

Thomas's remarkable and growing obsession with artefacts relied on an unusual paradigm — the changing physical characteristics of everyday eating utensils. After studying a broad array of forks, spoons, and knives during his first year at Cambridge, Thomas continued his research during the summer recess. In August, 1878, he travelled north to Sheffield, centre of Britain's cutlery industry. There, during four days of frenetic shopping, Thomas procured a wide range of eating implements, both new and used. While in Sheffield, he received some assistance from Mr. Robert Owen, Master Cutler at a local foundry. Thomas recorded each of his purchases in a small notebook, later submitted to his father for reimbursement.

Thomas's notebook, officially catalogued as the "Sheffield Notebook," is now part of the "Charles Darwin Collection" in the Cambridge University

Library. Roughly six inches in height and four inches in width, with unlined paper and a greenish, worn cloth cover, it is amongst similar "reimbursement" notebooks submitted to Charles Darwin by Thomas's siblings. Typically, the expenses viewed as appropriate for their father's compensation were either incurred on trips, most often to London to visit relatives, or related to the acquisition of texts and academic supplies, such as Thomas's purchase of a microscope in 1877. Charles Darwin filed each of these notebooks in his account book of the relevant year, and these ledgers (1839 to 1881, inclusive) are also preserved in the "Darwin Collection" at Cambridge.

The expense entries in the "Sheffield Notebook," along with accompanying observations and what appear to be six hastily drawn illustrations, are as follows:[15]

Sheffield

August 2nd, 1878 —
(1) Procured from the Owen foundry a large oyster ?? fork-spoon. Length from end to end 8", girth ½". Examined it with the Master Cutler, Mr. Robert Owen. It was there left stranded by a dissipated

---

15. Each illustration's approximate location within the following transcription is indicated by [Fig.]

gentryman. A dull silver. Mostly free from use. Hence probably does not inhabit coastal England. The plebs differ whether it should be considered a fork or a spoon. 23 shillings. [Fig.]

(2) Small silver olive spoon, 5 ⅞". Towards one end of the specimen, a yellowish appearance, which upon further exam, appeared to be two rudimentary tines, and remnants of a small olive, possibly Greek. 30 shillings. [Fig.]

(3) Examined but did not purchase a large number of hollowware and serving pieces. Carving forks and knifes, etc.

August 3rd, 1878 —
(4) Found these [Fig.] in Burwash and Sons — 1 shilling sixpence each.

(5) A tremendous find! Hurrah, hurrah! A 44-piece bride's set — 16 teaspoons, 8 place forks, 8 place knifes, 8 salad forks, sugar spoon, butter knifes, tablespoon, pierced tablespoon, and chest. Also a number of singular pieces — flat server and large cold meat fork. Successful bid — £9.6.2.

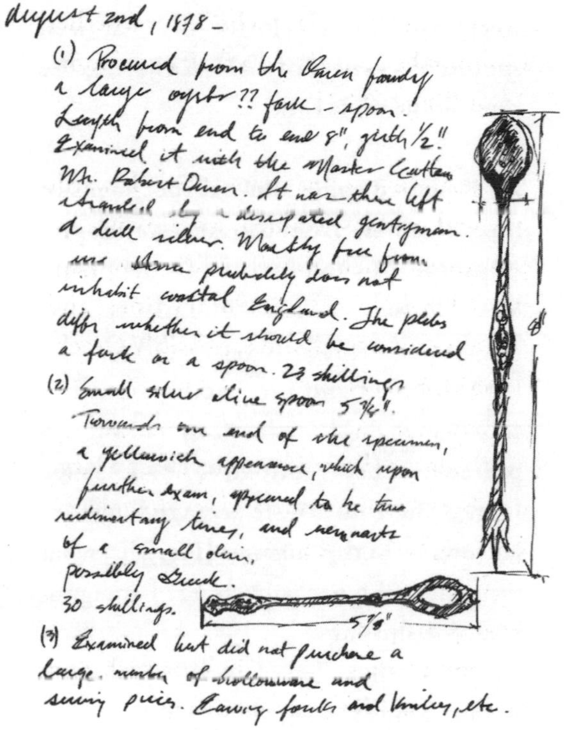

August 2nd, 1878 —

(1) Procured from the Owen foundry
a large oyster?? fork - spoon.
Length from end to end 8", girth ½".
Examined it with the Master Cutler
Mr. Robert Owen. It was there left
stranded by a disappeared gentleman.
A dull silver. Mostly free from
use. Stone probably does not
inhabit coastal England. The plebs
differ whether it should be considered
a fork or a spoon. 23 shillings.

(2) Small silver olive spoon 5⅜".
Towards one end of the specimen,
a yellowish appearance, which upon
further exam, appeared to be two
rudimentary tines, and remnants
of a small olive,
possibly Greek.
30 shillings.

(3) Examined but did not purchase a
large number of hollowware and
serving pieces. Carving forks and knives, etc.

Figure 7. A Facsimile from Thomas Darwin's
"Sheffield Notebook."

August 4th, 1878 —

(6) An observation — When scattered freely within the clutter of a drawer, spoons of a variety of makes adhere to the tines of the table fork.

(7) Procured some unusual specimens of the <illegible> from the antique shop of <illegible>. I soon perceived <illegible>. 50 shillings.

(8) Examined and procured a utensil of this shape [Fig.] — the tines had the appearance of being united, & of an ? shape [Fig.]. The 4 tines were arranged in regular rows — in this manner [Fig.]. To what name does this utensil belong? I am ignorant.[16] 8 shillings.

August 5th, 1878 —

(9) Today purchased a good many dessert forks — all manufactured in 1870 under the trademark Joseph Rogers & Sons, Ltd. Composition — silver plate? Without the aid of a microscope, I could perceive no

---

16. The utensil in question was a ramekin (also referred to as ramequin) fork. It was particularly useful for eating custard from small individual baking dishes, also known as ramekins (or ramequins).

differences. Yet when highly magnified, the tines were seen to have occasional imperfections. That such apparently identical utensils had distinctive marks warrants further investigation. £8.5.4.

(10) I found also another <illegible>. 6 shillings.

The following line of marginalia is also found within the notebook: "Owen - rahnd ended knoife." It seems Thomas was taken with Owen's pronunciation of what was presumably a round-ended knife and wished to record at least one example of the distinctive Sheffield dialect he encountered during his stay.

Due to a number of illegible entries, Thomas's exact outlay while in Sheffield is difficult to determine. However, an August 10th, 1878, entry of £30 in Charles Darwin's ledger and linked to Thomas's name almost certainly corresponds to these expenditures. Although Thomas's scrawl likely exasperated his father, Charles would not have begrudged the incurred expenses. Charles and Emma were highly supportive when it came to matters of their children's education or scholarly interests. Based on Charles's ledger entries, Thomas received a generous allowance of £100 per term throughout his two Cambridge undergraduate years. This amount was in addition to those quarterly bills Charles Darwin paid by cheque directly to the bursar at Christ's College. Although not itemized, these would have covered such costs as tuition, books, chamber (or room) rent, meals, and various outlays to tradespeople and college servants.

Thomas returned to Cambridge for his second year of studies in early October 1878. Aside from his participation in the *Plinian Society*, Thomas again seems to have avoided almost all formal courses and lectures. Instead, Thomas studied his "Sheffield" purchases intensely. The series of dessert forks provided him with what he considered unexpected and interesting morphologic data, while three unusual "specimens" ultimately became case studies in the extraordinary document he submitted to *Nature*. The manuscript, titled "Hybrid Artefacts and Their Role in Our Understanding of the Evolution of Inanimate Objects," was rejected, albeit with some consternation on the editor's part (see Chapters 6 to 8 for reproductions and discussion of his "artefact" manuscripts).

There is one additional account that concerns Thomas's experiences at Cambridge. Mr. Louis Ainsley, an amateur naturalist and self-proclaimed gourmand,[17] wrote an autobiographical sketch (*Looking Back*, by Louis Ainsley, printed for private circulation in 1930) that includes reminiscences of his stu-

---

17. While at Cambridge, Mr. Ainsley was a founding member of the Gourmet Club, whose members prided themselves on eating exotic birds and beasts. It may have been Mr. Ainsley's influence that accounted for the unusual course of Hawk and Bit-

dent days at Cambridge, which partially overlapped those of his fellow undergraduate, Thomas Darwin. Mr. Ainsley was also a member of the *Plinian Society*, joining at the beginning of the Michaelmas term in 1878. After first commenting upon a number of the *Society's* other members, he turned his attention to Thomas.

> Perhaps the strangest member that year was a Thomas Darwin, son of the renowned Charles Darwin, whom the majority of our little Society held with some awe and reverence since he had graced the Society with his presence the preceding year. From Thomas's demeanour, however, one would have never guessed his illustrious lineage. He was a quiet, shy individual, strangely distractible and preoccupied, who yet could become quite animated during serious discussion. Surprisingly, despite a voice that could occasionally pierce like a pigeon's, he was the best reader-aloud of our group. I recall his interests as unusual, aligned in some way to the Historical Sciences.

---

tern served at the *Plinian Society's* "Grand Dinner" in honour of (an unnamed) Monsieur. The Gourmet Club was disbanded in 1881 when three members almost died after devouring an old brown owl.

There was something remarkably odd yet appealing about Thomas, perhaps the eccentric enthusiasm beneath his outer crust, and I would have liked to have struck up a friendship. However, the meetings of the Society were conducted rather formally and exchanges were largely confined to the papers under discussion. It was only afterwards, when most of the members dined together in the evening (rousing good-natured affairs!) that true friendships emerged, often over "mild" games of vingt-et-un. I recall Thomas joining us on only one such occasion (as I believe he was conducting some experiment that required his nightly attention) and so he remained little known to us.

This singular evening was memorable, as a visitor from France was in attendance, and the Society hosted an elaborate dinner in his honour, one that I helped orchestrate. Although I have now forgotten the name of Monsieur, our menu, served à la français, remains a cherished memento. It is with particular amusement that I recall the oysters and how Venn suffered — not knowing which end of his implement to use to extract the

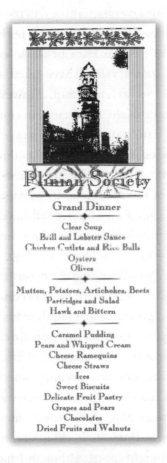

Plinian Society

Grand Dinner
◆
Clear Soup
Brill and Lobster Sauce
Chicken Cutlets and Rice Balls
Oysters
Olives
◆
Mutton, Potatoes, Artichokes, Beets
Partridges and Salad
Hawk and Bittern
◆
Caramel Pudding
Pears and Whipped Cream
Cheese Ramequins
Cheese Straws
Ices
Sweet Biscuits
Delicate Fruit Pastry
Grapes and Pears
Chocolates
Dried Fruits and Walnuts

Figure 8. Menu Card Used for the *Plinian Society*'s
Grand Dinner, 1878

delicious morsels.

There was one other awkward moment as well. At the end of the evening, Thomas was to thank Monsieur on behalf of the Society. He had apparently rehearsed a short speech and was quite animated as he mouthed what appeared to be an eloquent merci. Yet not a single word was uttered out loud. Although unsettled, we all applauded, as did the gracious Monsieur, and then Thomas sat down, satisfied and oblivious to his odd behaviour.

Venn was a reference to John Venn, then an enthusiastic "fresher" or first-year undergraduate. In the context of studying head growth, Venn went on to make yearly measurements of the length and breadth of the heads of all University of Cambridge students. The results, that brains continued to increase in size throughout the undergraduate years, were later to suggest to Francis Galton that brains could expand with exercise, an observation he published in the journal *Nature*. This odd inference, unknown to Thomas, would prove eerily similar to Thomas's speculations concerning the impact of exercise-like activity on the cutting tine of the dessert fork.

Following his second year at Cambridge, Thomas broke with family tradition and did not return to Down House for the summer academic recess. On June 9th, 1879, his mother visited him in Cambridge. Although the expressed intent of Emma's trip was to assist Thomas with "end-of-term" packing, both Emma and Charles had become increasingly uneasy over the state of Thomas's health. It was only upon Emma's arrival in Cambridge that she learned Thomas's summer plans had changed. Until then, he appears to have informed no one that he intended to travel to North America. Emma's concerned impressions of her son, as well as speculations about the possible intention of his North American trip and his "preoccupations," are recorded in a letter later sent to the London Asylum by a regretful Charles Darwin on behalf of his wife and himself (see Chapter 9).

The day after his mother's visit, Thomas travelled alone by train to Liverpool. As his parents were later to learn, Thomas then purchased steamship and rail tickets from Allan Brothers & Co., a Liverpool ticket agency, and on June 11th boarded the *Peruvian*. This steamship was part of a weekly Liverpool–Quebec passenger and cargo service operated by the Allan Line of Royal Mail Steamers. At the time, at 3038 tons and 400 feet long, the vessel was one of the fastest plying the North Atlantic. After calling at Londonderry to take on additional passengers and mail, the *Peruvian*'s trans-Atlantic crossing took just over seven days.

Thomas's time aboard the *Peruvian* can only be

surmised but was likely comfortable. His stateroom would have been stylishly equipped with bed and toilette appliances. First-class passengers also had exclusive access to the saloon (furnished with a pianoforte), the library, and an adjoining sitting room and smoking lounge. The saloon was also where communal meals were served, with the Allan line emphasizing in their promotional material that meals were presented *à la russe*. Familiar with this manner of dining only by reputation, Thomas may have been intrigued with the elaborate individual place settings this sequential style of service would have entailed. Etiquette then dictated there could be no more than three distinct knives and forks on the table for each passenger at any one time, although the oyster fork was excepted from such calculations.

FOUR

LONDON ASYLUM

On June 20th, 1879, the *Toronto Mail* carried the following story:

A DISTURBANCE AT GRAND TRUNK RAILWAY STATION

An incident occurred earlier today at Grand Trunk Railway Station. A young male was apprehended by police as dangerous to others and transported to the Toronto Gaol. According to Detective Heenan, three local officers, having being alerted by telegraph, boarded a train from Quebec City on its arrival in Toronto whereupon an agitated passenger was quickly seized. Detective Heenan reports a Mr. Darwin is now in custody at the Toronto Gaol where he is charged with committing a disturbance and uttering threats and indecent accusations. He is to undergo medical and judicial examinations for insanity.

At that time in Canada, those imprisoned who were also deemed to be insane could be transferred by a court-approved Lieutenant-Governor's Warrant to an asylum for involuntary confinement. As there was little tolerance for those who were disruptive in the penal system, the bureaucratic exigencies were dealt with swiftly. Only twelve days passed between the date of Thomas's gaol detention and the date of his conveyance by bailiff to the London Asylum. Although there were similar asylums in Toronto, Kingston, and Hamilton, admissions to these more crowded institutions occurred less frequently and depended upon the death or discharge of an existing patient.

The procedural aspects of obtaining a Lieutenant-Governor's Warrant involved one judicial and two medical opinions, all three subsequently reviewed by the Department of the Provincial Secretary. The two medical opinions, one of which was completed by the gaol surgeon, were to be conducted on separate occasions and were to distinguish between those facts personally observed and those facts, if any, communicated by others. Likely because the remuneration was so poor, most medical opinions emerged after very cursory examinations and amounted to little more than signed statements that the detained individual was insane. In Thomas's case, the gaol surgeon, a Dr. M. Nichol, certified on June 24th, 1879, "That he is insane in the expression of his countenance, manner, and conversations. Indifferent to all questions and talks only of forks and spoons." Dr. R. H. Clark's certificate, also signed on June 24th, 1879, was only marginally more detailed: "His talk suggests mental delusions and insanity. He imagines cutlery capable of independent life. He excitedly walks about his cell and is in a great state of agitation. Detective Heenan says he has been in his present state since leaving Quebec."

As a counterbalance to the often rash conclusions of the physicians, the process for providing judicial opinions was designed to be more rigorous. These required the completion of a schedule ("Schedule No. 2") that contained nineteen questions addressing basic identifying data, including the address of nearest relatives; the salient details of the "present attack" and its possible precipitating causes; the medical status of the "Prisoner;" and whether any funds were available "to contribute to the maintenance of the Prisoner while in an asylum."[18]

On June 26th, 1879, Thomas's "Schedule No. 2" was completed by a Justice R. M. Stephenson. Although Justice Stephenson conducted a full enquiry, the answers to most questions were recorded as "Unknown." It was unknown, for example, whether this was Thomas's first attack, whether he was subject to bodily ailments or to epilepsy or paralysis, and

18. Schedule No. 2: Information to be Elicited Upon Enquiry of a Person Charged with Being Insane (Under Sections 19 and 20, Chapter 220 of the Revised Statutes).

whether other members of his family may "have suffered in a similar way" or could contribute to Thomas's maintenance.

Justice Stephenson did establish some details related to the nature and circumstances of Thomas's acute presentation. Based on extracted comments from "Schedule No. 2," the duration of Thomas's present attack was: "At least throughout the last two days." The insanity was stated to show itself by: "Strange actions and talk aboard train. Would not leave dining car until removed." In response to the question of "Whether any Delusions, and if so, what are they?" it was noted that Thomas: "Talks about forks and spoons as if alive." The most consequential question on "Schedule No. 2" was Question 10, "Whether the Prisoner is suicidal or dangerous to others?" Justice Stephenson's recorded response was as follows: "Dangerous to others — yes. Takes great umbrage when challenged on his delusions. Police were threatened."

According to the following handwritten addendum at the bottom of the schedule, Justice Stephenson had relied on Detective Heenan as the source for the above information, limited as it was: "The above examination was this way taken in oath by me from Detective Heenan, the Prisoner's arresting officer — the Prisoner being too agitated to respond to most questions and no known family or other informants available — at Toronto this 26th day of June 1879 —

Justice R.M. Stephenson."

With Thomas viewed as dangerous, and therefore unfit to be at large, the authorities would have had little choice but to proceed to a Lieutenant-Governor's Warrant. The unhappy consequences followed quickly. Under the subsequent care of Dr. Richard M. Bucke, Medical Superintendent, Thomas's tragic confinement within the London Asylum spanned just under four months, from July 2nd to October 23rd, 1879. The documents immediately available to Bucke were of little value in accounting for Thomas's apparently rapid deterioration on arriving in Canada, and he would only later learn in a letter from Charles Darwin that Thomas had been unwell for at least one year prior to his asylum admission.

The most tangible evidence for Thomas's disordered thinking was an unusual manuscript he submitted to *Nature* just prior to departing for North America (see Chapter 8). Although Bucke did not have access to this document, his interviews with Thomas soon elicited its central thesis — Thomas's remarkable conviction that eating utensils mated with one another of their own volition, siring offspring that shared the physical characteristics of the two parents. Thomas was certain that these activities occurred without human intervention or assistance, his evidence being a number of unusual specimens, which he termed *hybrids*.

As it happened, Thomas had a more sympathetic

Figure 9. Thomas Darwin's Admission Medical Opinions and Schedule No. 2: Information to be Elicited Upon Enquiry of a Person Charged with Being Insane (Under Sections 19 and 20, Chapter 220 of the Revised Statutes)

ear in Dr. Bucke than might have been expected, due to the doctor's own idiosyncratic applications of Charles Darwin's evolutionary theories. These notions were the basis for numerous papers, essays, and addresses authored by Bucke and most comprehensively described in two of his books, *Man's Moral Nature* (1879) and *Cosmic Consciousness* (1901). In *Man's Moral Nature*, published just prior to Thomas's admission to the London Asylum and discussed in detail later in this volume, Bucke included proof of man's moral evolution by means of natural selection.

In his later book *Cosmic Consciousness*, Bucke argued that man had progressed from simple consciousness to self-consciousness and was on the verge of a new level of awareness which Bucke termed cosmic consciousness — a profound appreciation "of the life and order of the universe."[19] *Cosmic Consciousness* ended on the optimistic note that the incidence of those attaining cosmic consciousness was increasing, and Bucke forecast that, with time, cosmic insight would become universal.

Although Thomas's surname and British birthplace were noted on his transfer documents from the Toronto Gaol, Bucke at first doubted Thomas's

19. Bucke believed there were fourteen certain and thirty-six possible cases of individuals with demonstrated cosmic consciousness. Modestly, Bucke included himself within the "possible" category.

apparent parentage. His mistrust stemmed from a misdiagnosis that occurred two years prior to Thomas's admission. Bucke's appointment at the London Asylum was on the basis of political patronage, rather than any expertise or even aptitude. When he first arrived as a novice medical superintendent at the London Asylum in 1877, Bucke had virtually no psychiatric training and was remarkably naive. One of his first patients with mania presented with a grandiose delusion that she was a relative of Queen Victoria and convinced Bucke to petition for her release directly to Ontario's Provincial Secretary. This proved to be an enormous political embarrassment, and Bucke was harshly chastised by Inspector J. W. Langmuir to whom he directly reported.

Langmuir's rebuke is documented in a letter to Bucke dated October 17th, 1877: "The Victoria affair is hopefully behind us. You are now to diagnose as follows: those who cry are melancholic, those who laugh are manic. The rest are not to be believed." Thereafter, Bucke rarely took information conveyed by his patients at face value. He became a cautious diagnostician and relied on repeated interviews before proceeding on the basis of the information presented to him. Understandably, Bucke was particularly leery of those patients who claimed famous identities or associations to famous personages. It therefore took time for Bucke to appreciate Thomas's true pedigree and then attempt to contact his father, particularly as Thomas appears to have been more interested in professing his theories than in recounting his personal background.

One additional explanation for the initial uncertainty regarding Thomas's background may have been the extent of Bucke's fascination with Walt Whitman. Bucke had begun to worship the American poet in 1872, after an evening of reading Whitman's poems inspired an epiphany in which he experienced the living presence of the Cosmos. Bucke, largely viewed as a sycophant by serious Whitman scholars, subsequently met Whitman on a number of occasions and eventually invited the poet to observe his patients at the London Asylum.[20] Bucke's passionate devotion "was so intense and of such long standing that over the years he came to look like Whitman. Sometimes he even fancied he was Whitman." Photographs leave

---

20. Walt Whitman visited the London Asylum in the summer of 1880 and subsequently left these poignant observations, "The wonderful phenomena of lunacy — what does that mean? Has it a physical basis? Or physical entanglements? Or what: It is a lesson to see Bucke's asylum at London — the hundreds on hundreds of his insane. I used to wander through the wards quite freely — go everywhere — even among the boisterous patients — the very violent. But I couldn't stand it long — I finally told Doctor I could not continue to do it. I think I gave him back the key which he had entrusted to me: It became a too-near-fact — too poignant — too sharply painful — too ghastly true." Shortt, *Victorian Lunacy* (Cambridge: Cambridge University Press, 1986).

Figure 10. Dr. Richard Maurice Bucke

Figure 11. Mr. Walt Whitman

little doubt that Bucke went to great lengths to achieve a Whitmanesque presence. Given the porous nature of Bucke's own fragile personae, he appreciated that patients such as Thomas might likewise appropriate the identities and pedigrees of others.

Despite their mutual intellectual interests, Bucke viewed Thomas as quietly but seriously disturbed throughout his entire admission. Fortunately for Thomas, the year 1879 coincided with a phase in Bucke's career in which his therapeutic approach was conservative. Had Thomas encountered Bucke earlier he would have been at real risk of receiving the surgical treatment for masturbatory insanity. Bucke's attack on "the solitary vice," then presumed to be ubiquitous in all male patients, was the surgical insertion of a "silver wire" through the prepuce or foreskin, which was designed to interfere with the potential and pleasure of self-abuse.

Two years prior to Thomas's admission, nineteen male patients at the London Asylum underwent the "wiring" procedure. Fortunately, Bucke reviewed the effectiveness of his surgical program and found the clinical status of most patients was unchanged. In view of the technical challenges of the procedure, as well as the (not surprising!) degree of patient opposition, Bucke wisely cancelled the program.

Instead, Bucke returned to advocating the conventional virtues of work, constructive amusement, and prayer. A note in Bucke's diary indicates that

Thomas was assigned to the Asylum's gardening crew. In addition to tending acres of root vegetables, Thomas would also have cared for an impressive variety of flowers that grew in the ornamental gardens surrounding the main buildings.

As for the "Constructive Amusements," Thomas presumably attended what were known as "Entertainments." Held every two to three weeks, these were itemized each year in Bucke's annual report. During the period of Thomas's confinement, seven concerts and dramatic performances took place, most involving some combination of the Asylum's Dramatic Club, the Asylum's Junior Dramatic Club, and the Asylum Band. There were also biweekly evening poetry recitals and two trips outside the institution, one to a visiting circus, and the other to a public fireworks display.

The indoor entertainments were held in the "Amusement Room," located up three flights of stairs on the top-most floor of the Asylum's main building. As there was no chapel on the Asylum's grounds, this large room was also where religious services took place. During the period of Thomas's confinement, there were three separate services held every Sunday: a Roman Catholic Mass at nine a.m., a Presbyterian service at ten-thirty a.m., and mid-afternoon prayers conducted by Church of England clergy. To relieve the horrible tedium of asylum life, many of the patients attended all three services. As the amusement room also contained a billiards table, Thomas may have been attracted by the games the patients would play before and after each service.

The religious pluralism proved problematic. As the provincial Inspector of Asylums, Prisons, and Public Charities, part of Inspector Langmuir's responsibilities was to conduct frequent inspections of each asylum in Ontario and to present the findings to the Ontario Legislative Assembly in an annual report. As it was Langmuir's enlightened custom to speak in confidence to as many patients as possible during his inspections, he invariably documented numerous complaints, most of which were frivolous and undeserved. However, Langmuir was not averse to further investigation and would ameliorate any complaint he felt represented a justifiable concern.

Following his September 1879 inspection, Langmuir recorded that a number of patients complained of proselytizing ministers and aggressive efforts to effect conversions. As a result, Langmuir ordered that, effective immediately, patients could only attend the weekly service of their respective denomination. Bucke ensured that the Catholic and Presbyterian services were limited to the declared members of their faiths. However, as the son of a Church of England cleric, Bucke quietly allowed the afternoon ministrations of his own priest to remain open to all patients.

Langmuir also noted three other concerns worthy of investigation during his September 1879 inspection. The most prevalent complaint was insufficient food. After establishing that the weight of most patients had increased since their admissions, Langmuir felt it unnecessary to adjust serving portions. As a gesture of goodwill, Langmuir did instruct that gooseberry preserves for all patients were to be introduced at the evening meal.

The Asylum's alcohol policy also raised significant ire. Although alcohol had been prescribed in enormous quantities prior to his arrival, Bucke introduced an abstinence policy, citing unanimous patient support. Langmuir heard otherwise, but felt compelled to support Bucke's directive. He did reinstate, however, the evening orange posset[21] for the Asylum medical staff.

Lastly, there were those who were disappointed with the poetry evenings. These had become monotonous affairs, in which Bucke read only selections from Whitman's *Leaves of Grass*. A sympathetic Langmuir, aware of Bucke's infatuation with Whitman as well as his dull style of recitation, permitted the evenings to continue provided Bucke also allowed others to read poems of their choosing.

Though the introduction of gooseberry preserve is suggestive, there is no indication whether

<hr>

21. A cream-based drink curdled with sweet wine and flavoured with orange extract.

Thomas actually met Langmuir and, if he had, whether he voiced similar or additional complaints to those noted above. It seems reasonable to assume that Thomas's greatest concern during his confinement, aside from its involuntary nature, was with Bucke himself. In a letter Thomas wrote to his mother (see Chapter 10), apparently the only one written during his confinement, he described Bucke as "villainous," and indifferent to his staff's abusive behaviour. In contradiction, Thomas also complained to his mother that his visits with Bucke were too short, implying at least some desire for more than their brief contact.

Approximately two months into the course of his confinement, a note in Bucke's diary indicates that Thomas was transferred from the main building of the Asylum, which lodged the vast majority of patients, to one of the three much smaller, free standing, residential cottages, each lodging sixty patients. Although this meant greater liberty for Thomas, his move to new accommodation was portentous. The cottages were reserved for the "quiet" chronic cases and, by inference, Thomas's prognosis was viewed as poor.

Nevertheless, Thomas's new setting was better, or at least more tranquil, than the "refractory ward," another segregated building which housed "the very violent, the very dirty, and those who are determined to elope if possible, and who have considerable ingenuity available for this purpose." As one new priv-

Figure 12. Playing Croquet in the Garden
at the London Asylum.

ilege, Thomas gained considerable access to the Asylum grounds. Here he would have met other patients in relatively favourable circumstances and possibly even participated in various recreational activities, such as the then popular game of croquet.

Thomas was also now afforded an opportunity to borrow books from a lending library. With Bucke's encouragement, Thomas read *Man's Moral Nature* although, as Bucke's diary indicates, he found its inherent logic unsatisfactory. Unfortunately, it soon became evident to Bucke that Thomas was extremely ill with tuberculosis, a disease that then lacked effective treatment and could progress rapidly. Ironically, it was likely the Asylum's own cows, milked by the patients, which carried and transmitted the tubercle bacillus.

Despite the efforts of Dr. William Osler, "a young gentleman of great name and of promise unfulfilled" died in the London Asylum on October 23rd, 1879. Due to Bucke's intervention, Thomas's final letter to his mother was never delivered.

PART TWO

COLLECTED WORKS

FIVE

SPECIES AND VARIETIES

By the time Thomas Darwin attended Cambridge, he had carefully read *On the Origin of Species* and deeply admired its contents. The work had first been published by his father in November 1859, some two years after Thomas's birth. Ironically, the book emerged as a precipitous act of composition after more than twenty years of Charles Darwin's plodding and methodical efforts to collect evidence in support of his evolutionary theories. Until then, his insights had been expounded in private notebooks and various letters to colleagues but remained unpublished, despite repeated entreaties by associates to do so. The impetus for the belated appearance of *On the Origin of Species* was a brief essay that Alfred Wallace, a young naturalist, had forwarded to Charles Darwin for his review. In the midst of a high fever while in Ternate in the Malay Archipelago, Wallace had suddenly realized what Darwin felt tediously compelled to prove: the pivotal role of the struggle for existence as a mechanism for evolutionary change.

An awkward Charles Darwin, embarrassed to

discover that he wished to be recognized as the original theorist, was uncertain how to proceed. Darwin elected to forward Wallace's essay to Sir Charles Lyell with a favourable recommendation for its immediate publication. Lyell, a long-standing colleague of Darwin, was aware that Darwin's similar but more detailed notions had preceded those of Wallace. With the assistance of Joseph Hooker, Lyell diplomatically arranged to have Wallace's essay and selections of Darwin's earlier work simultaneously read at a meeting of the *London Linnean Society* on July 1st, 1858. Darwin's more comprehensive studies were published as *On the Origin of Species* just over one year later, although from his perspective, still in imperfect "Abstract" form and less detailed than originally intended.

On the Origin of Species began with Darwin's "collection and observation of a great many specimens showing that offspring tend to vary in many minor ways from their parent stock." Building upon Malthus's insight that "many more individuals of each species are born than can possibly survive," Darwin concluded that the survivors were those whose variations were advantageously adapted to local conditions. "This preservation of favourable individual differences and variations, and the destruction of those which are injurious, I have called Natural Selection, or the Survival of the Fittest."

Charles Darwin's conceptual framework of evolution, in his words — "one long argument" — was not without flaws. His theory on use and disuse, by which "use in our domestic animals has strengthened and enlarged certain parts, and disuse diminished them," included Lamarck's now discredited notion that such acquired modifications could be inherited. This, Charles Darwin would later theorize, occurred by a process he termed *pangenesis*, which involved the supposed transfer of representative particles, or *gemmules*, from all the organs and tissues of the body to the gonads and germ cells.[22] It was not until the rediscovery in 1900 of Gregor Mendel's botanical experiments, published in the 1860s but initially ignored, that a more accurate notion of genes and heredity emerged.

Despite these missteps, Darwin's revolutionary insights were earth-shaking. Yet, *On the Origin of Species* received a mixed reception, nowhere more so than within the Darwin household. Charles Darwin's theories were in direct conflict with the orthodox Christian belief that each species was created independently by divine intervention. Emma Darwin, devoutly religious, became convinced that her husband's religious disbelief, an unavoidable blasphemous consequence of his scientific theories, was the source of his chronic illness. Concerned about the eternal implications for Charles, Emma begged

22. As presented in his 1868 work *The Variation of Animals and Plants under Domestication*.

Figure 13. Emma Darwin

her husband to pray for the sake of his health.

Though neither Emma nor Charles aggressively courted their children in the ensuing struggle between science and religion within their household, Thomas was unavoidably caught in the unspoken conflict. Respectful of both his parents' views, Thomas allowed Sunday, a day of various Sabbath prohibitions in the Darwin home, to belong to his mother. On weekdays throughout his adolescence, however, Thomas assisted with his father's assorted experiments, took dictation, dissected specimens, read correspondence out loud, and provided rough illustrations for various scientific writings. Versed first in his father's manner of working, and then in his ideas, Thomas quickly began to extend the latter.

Thomas's immediate source of inspiration at Cambridge was the work of Lieutenant-General Augustus Henry Pitt Rivers (original surname Lane Fox), a pioneering anthropologist whose artefact collections included not only Australian Aboriginal weapons but also archaeological relics found on his estates in the British Isles. After retiring from the military, Pitt Rivers lectured at Cambridge, selecting items from his Australian armaments to display how simple weapons had slowly progressed to more complex entities. These demonstrations were critical to Thomas's new intellectual direction, as evidenced by the following letter to his father.

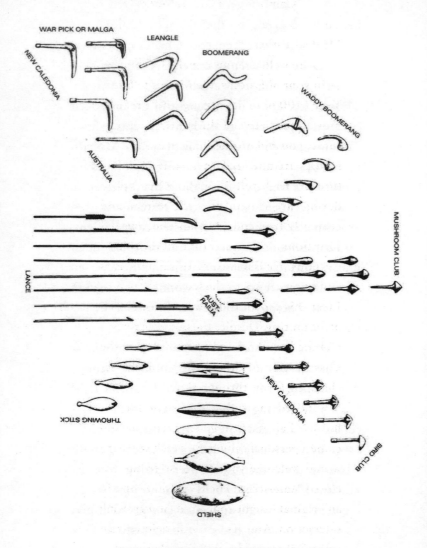

**Figure 14. Pitt Rivers's Collection of
Australian Aboriginal Weapons**

My dear Father,

I am well and now equally well settled — in your old rooms, the Master tells me. Your £100 note has arrived and I remain most appreciative of the generous opportunity you and Mother have provided. My studies are now in earnest, although lectures are frightfully dull. Pitt Rivers's ponderings are as painful as the others, and currently I am enduring his laborious descriptions of Australian Aboriginal weapons. He is unwise to bring his spears and boomerangs to the lecture theatre — I fear this provocation may yet lead to violent mutiny. Despite these complaints, I feel the keenest delight in pondering the classification of these weapons and their changing forms through time.

Indeed, the study of the origin and evolution of artefacts in general has now become a personal calling. So much so, that I would welcome your response to the enclosed Manuscript. I believe it may contain an original insight concerning a surprising interaction. And yes — it is in deference to your advice to study some special group that I have, after deliberation, selected our everyday eating utensils to represent my special world of inanimate objects.

In Pitt Rivers's lectures, a particular dissatisfaction of mine relates to his distinctions between one weapon and the next — what he calls a throwing stick, I might as easily have named a lance or war club. In considering this matter, I believe a more sophisticated taxonomy needs to be adopted. You will recognize my decision — the terms of classification utilized in the Manuscript are those borrowed from Linnaeus and Lyell. In the world of artefacts, however, I have deemed a species to be an entity that differs from other species by function — that is, by what it docs. In contrast, varieties of the same species are distinguished by form.

I therefore consider the fork and spoon, each with a recognizable function quite dissimilar from the other, as two distinct species; whereas the dinner fork, the salad fork and, as I now appreciate, a remarkable range of other specialized forks, I view as varieties.

In closing, Father, be well. You will have detected the Manuscript's inspiration — I hope you are not displeased. In rereading On the Origin of Species, I was much struck that its elegant observations and theories appear to throw light on my new-found world. Give my love to Mother, to little Bernard, to Polly, to sisters, brothers, and of course to all relations. I await your sage comments on taxonomy. If you concur, I plan to read the Manuscript at an upcoming meeting of the Plinian Society.

Your Loving Son,

Thomas

Post Script — Father, remember the two Roman coins and the short report Horace and I undertook? Remember how we felt that one of the coins was far older than the other? And remember how their images were similar but different? I now wonder whether the successive images of these types of coins were determined by certain laws, perhaps analogous to those by which the successive forms of animals and plants appear to be governed.

Charles was no doubt pleased to receive his son's letter. In addition to hearing from Thomas — a rare, if not singular, event — a young scientist was seeking his advice. Perhaps sensing that the timing was propitious, Charles responded immediately and included comments about his own approach to scholarly investigation.

Down, Monday Morning, 8:30 A.M.
[October 23rd, 1877]

My dear Thomas,

Your letter dated 17th October arrived in yesterday's post. Your mother and I must exhort you to write more — it is such a pleasure to read your words! And though I am sorry to learn your low opinion of the current lectures, I am not surprised. It would appear that in some matters, evolution may proceed far too slowly.

But on to your new-found world! First, you must hear how pleased I am to learn you have joined (I have surmised this is so) the Plinian Society. I am confident you will find the Society a most useful and supportive environment. I recall fondly the first paper I read to that venerable gathering.[23] Its far too generous reception was instrumental in stimulating my zeal for a scholarly life — a desire I am delighted to see that you so obviously and tangibly share.

I am, of course, now referring to your Manuscript — a compelling work and one

23. Charles Darwin reported "that the so-called ova of Flustra had the power of independent movement by means of cilia, and were in fact larvae." *Autobiography*, Darwin, C. (New York: Dover Publications, 1958) 13, 14.

you should not hesitate to present. The comments from colleagues will be helpful, and as you have sought my advice, I too will raise a few points you may wish to consider. I am flattered, by the way, that you have remembered and taken to heart my suggestion of studying "some special group" — a lesson learned after eight years with the — accursed! — Cirripedia.[24] You will see I am in a reflective mood, a keepsake of my — twice accursed! — "Recollections," now finished, provided I die immediately. Indeed, I am tempted to do so simply to avoid the tedious subject I must dissect.

And now on to your Manuscript. Though I am impressed with the theorizing power you demonstrate within it, there is room for the additional and detailed analysis of actual specimens. As yours is largely an historical narrative, I realize the problems inherent in such advice. Aside

---

24. Also known as barnacles. After eight years of tedious dissection, Charles Darwin eventually published his exhaustive findings describing both the living and extinct species. He was ambivalent about his obsessive devotion to the undertaking, alternating in the same paragraph between the work's "considerable value" and then doubting "whether the work was worth the consumption of so much time." *Autobiography*, Darwin, C. (New York: Dover Publications, 1958) 41.

from the dining room sideboard, the scullery, and your mother's cupboards, I am not entirely sure where contemporary eating utensils "reside," let alone their distant ancestors. Yet, I suspect there are estates, and shops, and museums, and collections, and catalogues, and factories, and cutlers — in short, a world of eating utensils, past and present, in both "domesticated" and "natural" states, not only to read about, but also to discover in actuality. Indeed, I envy you your unexplored world. But here I must lecture — do not indulge in the loose speculations so easily started by every smatterer and wandering collector.[25] Instead — first observe, then collect, and then catalogue. In time, and with reflection, sound theory and experimentation will follow.

As for the definition of "species," there are those who believe a distinct

---

25. Years earlier, Charles had advised his friend J.D. Hooker in similar fashion. Although Charles was emphasizing "observation" to Thomas, his own scientific method suggested a shift from observer to theorizer to experimentalist. Analysts such as Ernst Mayr tend to emphasize the unique convergence of all three traits within Charles Darwin as he matured as a scientist. (See Mayr, E. *One Long Argument: Charles Darwin and the Genesis of Modern Evolutionary Thought*. Questions of Science Series. Cambridge, Mass.: Harvard University Press, 1991.)

species can be defined primarily by morphologic characteristics — or by what you describe as form. From what you report, it appears that this is the approach adopted by Pitt Rivers. Nevertheless, as you imply, the differences in form sufficiently important to merit a specific species name are not always apparent. Your own emphasis on function rather than form is intriguing. The central function of both the carriage and the train might be considered the land transportation of goods — are they varieties of the same species? Perhaps, although I have a vague sense that each is more akin to a distinct species. But my stomach now begins to ache[26] — a signal that I must promptly leave these reflections.

In closing, Son, be well. I rejoice in your independent mind and your determination to make a contribution to the field of science. Further, I am impressed with the potential application of the evolutionary analogy to the world of artefacts,

---

26. Darwin was aware that his stomach pain could be precipitated by serious and concentrated intellectual effort, or as he put it, "I find the noodle and the stomach are antagonistic powers." *To Be an Invalid*, Colp, R. (Chicago: University of Chicago Press, 1977) 15.

provided fanciful analogies are not drawn. (Be aware, however, of the persecution and ridicule that awaits the public presentation of new ideas.) If I reflect on my own success as a man of science, whatever this may have amounted to, I believe it has largely been determined by these same mental qualities which you so amply possess. I hope this will be seen more as a comfort than a concern.

Hurrah for the forks and for the knives and for my son Thomas.

Your affectionate Father,

C. Darwin

Post Script — I too have mused about your ancient coins. Were they not found in a recently ploughed field? At the time, I remember that Horace, you, and I speculated about buried treasure. But I now suspect the coins were inadvertently dropped and gradually became covered by vegetable mould, courtesy of the earthworm and then were uncovered, courtesy of the plough. A more prosaic explanation but perhaps more likely. C. D.

**Post Post Script — A last thought. It oc-
curs to me that another example of a rudimentary character is the diminished sail
on board the new trans-Atlantic steamers.
You can see I am warming to the subject.
C. D.**

Charles was in a nostalgic mood. As he conveyed to Thomas, he had recently finished writing
his "Recollections," originally titled "Recollections
of the Development of My Mind and Character".
Charles had initiated the work after he had received
an editor's request for "an account of the development of my mind and character." As Charles felt that
the attempt might interest his descendants, his preliminary notes gradually expanded into a short
sketch of his life, one that he continued to supple-
ment up until the time of his death.

Perhaps Charles's recent work on his "success as
a man of science" had also reminded him of his own
lessons learnt regarding the vital importance of detailed analysis of actual specimens. Although
Charles advises Thomas that he still needs to un-
dertake such analyses in order to support his conjectures, he also expresses an enthusiastic and
genuine openness to his son's unusual ideas. Wisely
or unwisely, Charles's letter also gently prepares
Thomas for the "persecution and ridicule" that in-
vestigations in unexpected directions could incur, a

warning that would ultimately prove more prophetic than Charles could have anticipated.

As the manuscript that Thomas sent his father was evidently not preserved, it is unclear to what extent Thomas revised his original draft in response to the few specific suggestions his father provided. Although Thomas had sought particular advice on artefact taxonomy, especially assistance with definitions of species and varieties, his father's diffident comments were unlikely to have been helpful.[27]

Thomas did cite his father's example of the sail as a rudimentary character in his final manuscript. Charles's insight into viewing such sails as rudimentary characters may have been inspired by a well-publicized incident that occurred during an autumn 1877 trans-Atlantic crossing of the *Concordia*, a steam passenger liner whose twin-cylinder compound engine failed during its voyage. Fortunately, the ship then successfully proceeded under sail, eventually arriving safely at the port of St. John's, Newfoundland. Charles, a voracious newspaper

---

27. Charles Darwin was actually quite unclear throughout his career about the notion of species and speciation and frequently contradicted himself. He initially believed what is now the current consensus: that the central defining feature of a species is based on reproductive isolation and that distinct species do not interbreed with each other. He eventually concluded distinct species could be better defined primarily by unique characteristics in their physical form.

reader, likely would have read a number of accounts in *The Times* and relayed details of the affair to his family during their wide-ranging evening discussions. Otherwise, as the final version of Thomas's manuscript is still principally a narrative overview, his father's appeal for additional details of actual specimens appears to have been ignored.

SIX

RUDIMENTARY CHARACTERS

On February 2nd, 1878, Thomas Darwin read the following version of his manuscript to the *Plinian Society*. It represented Thomas's first contribution to his chosen field of scholarly endeavour. By "character," Thomas would be referring to any physical characteristic of the artefact in question.

ARTEFACTS AND THE ORIGIN OF THEIR RUDIMENTARY CHARACTERS: BY MEANS OF COMPETITION BETWEEN SPECIES

I have it on the good authority of my father that rudimentary organs bearing the plain stamp of inutility are extremely common, or even general, throughout nature. So, too, are characters in a rudimentary condition throughout the world of artefacts.

In the tobacco pipe, for instance, the protuberance at the bottom of the bowl was once much more developed than its current rudimentary form suggests. Originally broad at the bottom and flat, its early form allowed the bowl to rest upon the table, even as the pipe was being smoked. The protuberance has ceased being used in this fashion, and has in consequence become much reduced. Many similar instances of rudimentary characters could be given: the diminished sail of the trans-Atlantic steamers, even the attenuated designs on ancient British coins.

My father believes it probable that, throughout nature, disuse has been the main agent in rendering organs rudimentary; so too, I believe, in the world of artefacts. By small stages, disuse slowly leads to the further and further reduction of a character, until at last it becomes greatly atrophied. There remains, however, this fundamental difficulty: why does disuse occur? In considering this question, existing opinion has emphasized the vagaries of fashion. In the case of the tobacco pipe, the manner of smoking altered so that the pipe came to be continuously held. No longer placed upon a table, disuse of the bottom of its bowl ensued and thereby reduced the protuberance to its present rudimentary condition.

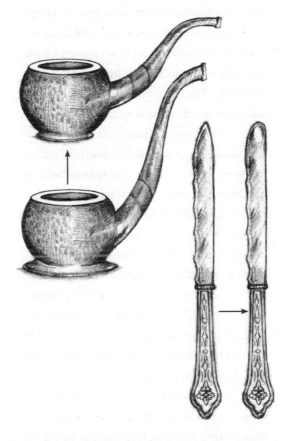

Figure 15. Rudimentary Characters (Illustrations by Thomas Darwin, from "Artefacts and the Origin of Their Rudimentary Characters: By Means of Competition Between Species," 1878).

I have come to recognize there is another mechanism as to why disuse occurs: the evolution of one species of artefact affects the evolution of another species. (And by species here I refer to an entity that differs from other entities by its function.)

Consider the table fork and its profound influence on the evolving shape of the table knife. Pitt Rivers informs us that sharp-edged flints for cutting and sharp-pointed sticks for spearing were the earliest eating utensils. Over time, a single "all-purpose" implement emerged — a knife whose blade contained both a sharp cutting edge and pointed tip. Yet, eating with only a single knife was difficult. Cutting meat required holding it steady with bread or, more often, the fingers of one's free hand. Although one could grasp a knife in each hand, a knife still failed as an effective "holding" device. A utensil with at least two pointed tips was required — consequently, the introduction of the two-pronged fork.

At first, forks were employed principally in the kitchen to aid carving and serving. But smaller versions of the kitchen fork gradually migrated to the table. With the table fork's superior ability to spear and hold food, the table knife's pointed tip became redundant. Disuse resulted, and the pointed table knife was slowly transformed into a blunt-nosed instrument.

In summary, the table knife and table fork have evolved in form due to their competition with one another. The table knife, originally serving two purposes, has had its pointed tip become much reduced due to competition with the table fork; yet the table knife's cutting edge remains perfectly efficient. We may conclude that competition between species can contribute to the existence of characters in a rudimentary condition.

Although it appears Thomas's reading was generally well-received, there were some who were confused by the additional instances of rudimentary characters that Thomas had provided. The *Society's* "minute-book" records of February 19th, 1878, read as follows:

"In a response to queries from a number of Society members, Mr. Thomas Darwin provided the following remarks: 'In my recent presentation to the Society, I offered that the diminished sail of a trans-

Atlantic steamer was an instance of a rudimentary character. By way of further explanation, the nineteenth century has marked the introduction of oceanic steam navigation. As the steam engine is as yet unreliable, sails continue to maintain a presence on the steamers, albeit with gradually diminishing size. Hence, today's diminutive sail can be viewed as a rudimentary character.

"In a similar fashion, the attenuated designs on ancient British coins also represent rudimentary states, but here the justification is more complex. First, coins are struck from the successive generations of engraved dies. Secondly, the art of engraving being imperfect, each generation of coins varies significantly from its predecessor. Thirdly, new dies are often copied from coins whose once detailed inscriptions have been faded by circulation. As a result, a complicated design tends to revert into a figure of much simpler execution. Here I refer members of the Society to illustrations found in an earlier work titled "Coinage of the Ancient Britons at Down" published in the London Numismatics Monthly Intelligencer in 1869. It will be seen that on the obverse of the more recent

of the coins, the head has been much reduced to a wreath. In similar fashion, on
the reverse of the more recent coin, only a
single horse remains from the earlier char-
iot and four horses. Hence, the testimony
of the coins speaks to the descent of characters to a rudimentary condition.'"

Thomas's clarification was accepted, and that
summer his original reading appeared in print in the
Transactions of the Plinian Society. Two sets of fig-
ures accompanied the published text, offering strong
visual corroboration that the bowl of the tobacco
pipe and the tip of the table knife survived only in
rudimentary form.

Initially, Charles Darwin must have been delighted that Thomas's observations had appeared in
print and were modelled so closely after his own arguments in *On the Origin of Species*.[28] Later, however,
Charles learned that it was Samuel Butler who had
first applied the term *rudimentary* to the tobacco
pipe's bowl in his novel *Erewhon* (1872). To be fair to
Thomas, Butler's satirical observation was merely the
starting point for Thomas's more complex and original insight. Moreover, by using the phrase "existing
opinion" within his manuscript, Thomas had referred
to the work of others, albeit generically. Nevertheless,

---

28. Indeed, Thomas employed a few phrases identical to
those written in *On the Origin of Species*!

Charles felt obliged to discuss with Thomas the importance of acknowledging one's debt to the scholarship of others.

Thomas's failure to cite Butler may have had unexpected repercussions. Following the publication of Thomas's work on rudimentary characters, Samuel Butler began to virulently accuse Charles of deriving his evolutionary views from Erasmus Darwin, Charles's grandfather.[29] Although Erasmus Darwin speculated about evolution in his earlier work *Zoonomia* (published in 1794), Butler's suggestion that he anticipated Charles Darwin's major theoretical advances was untrue. Samuel Butler's fury, heretofore inexplicable to so many historians, may have been a displaced response, incited by Thomas's failure to explicitly acknowledge the inspiration *Erewhon* had provided.

Charles Darwin refrained from replying publicly to Butler's accusations. However, in what he thought was the privacy of his autobiography,

---

29. Butler was not the first to wonder whether Charles Darwin had been ungenerous in acknowledging the views of Erasmus Darwin and other early evolutionists. In response to this criticism, Charles prefaced the third edition of *On the Origin of Species* (1861) with an essay titled "An Historical Sketch of the Recent Progress of Opinion on the Origin of Species." By the sixth edition (1872), the title of the essay further emphasized the temporal relationship of his work to earlier authors — "An Historical Sketch of the Progress of Opinion on the Origin of Species, Previously to the Publication of the First Edition of this Work."

Darwin's consoling description of his relationship to his tormentor was:

> *Hat doch der Wallfisch seine Laus*
> *Muss auch die Meine haben*

In English, the phrase would be roughly translated as "every apple has its worm."

Thomas Darwin's next scholarly endeavour was fuelled by a summer field trip. Following his initial year at Cambridge, and coinciding with the achievement of his first *Plinian Society* publication, Thomas returned to Down for the summer break. Possibly motivated by the promotional catalogues of various silverware manufacturers and dealers, he visited Sheffield at the beginning of August 1878.[30] The trip seems to have been a deliberate expedition to acquire as many species and varieties of eating utensils as he could find and that he felt his father could afford. Based on entries in the "Sheffield Notebook," Thomas's foraging was a success and he returned with a large collection.

---

30. Down House is now maintained by English Heritage as a memorial to Charles Darwin and is preserved as it stood in Victorian times. The catalogues from various silverware dealers that Thomas read that summer can still be found in its library as can many of the novels read by the family, including *The Ugly Duckling*. Thomas's two ancient British coins are also on view, wall-mounted in a small frame in his father's study.

In retrospect, Thomas's subsequent scientific plan becomes relatively clear. Forgoing most of his formal lectures, he spent much of his second year at Cambridge cataloguing his newly acquired pieces, studying in exquisite detail their morphology and taxonomy. It was a pastry fork that inspired his next publication. To Thomas, it illustrated the agency of increased use.

SEVEN

THE PASTRY FORK

The "minute-book" records of the *Plinian Society* show that on November 16th, 1878, "Mr. Thomas Darwin communicated to the *Society* an observation which he had made: That the pastry fork possesses a cutting tine due to the agency of increased use." Thomas's full communication is preserved within the spring 1879 issue of the *Transactions of the Plinian Society* and is reproduced here. Thomas's drawings accompanied the short report.

ON THE EFFECTS OF THE INCREASED USE OF A CHARACTER IN A DOMESTIC EATING UTENSIL

From the facts alluded to in a previous publication [see *Transactions of the Plinian Society* 8: 63–65, 1878], I think that there can be no doubt that disuse in our domestic artefacts has weakened and diminished certain characters; and that such modifications are sustained over time. Conversely, the increased use of a character may also have a marked influence on its morphology or form. In what follows I shall, for the sake of brevity, speak of the lower tine of the pastry fork (often referred to as its cutting tine) but it will be understood that a like argument is applicable to the agency of increased use of virtually any character of any artefact species in size, weight, capacity for performing a function, etc...

The specimen represented in Fig. A is a pastry fork of the Vintage pattern of silver plate, made sometime in the early 1870s by Joseph Rogers & Sons, Ltd. I am grateful to Mr. Robert Owen who assisted my acquisition of this piece this past summer. It will be appreciated, despite the artistic limitations of my illustration, that the pastry fork's distinctive morphology is defined by the obvious asymmetry of its four tines. If held in the right hand and at right angles to a table, the pastry fork's bottom-most or lowest tine is significantly wider and heavier than its three brethren except near its tip, which tapers rapidly on the inner side to preserve a sharpened point.

In now discussing the origins of the pastry fork, it is first necessary to recognize the historical change in dining fashion associated with the introduction of service *à la russe* (which arrived in England, according to Mr. Louis Ainsley, sometime in the mid-eighteen hundreds). As dishes are served in succession rather than all together, service *à la russe* established the dessert course as a distinct dénouement to the evening meal. Further, it has ensured that dessert is presented only after previous courses have been cleared, and that fresh eating utensils accompany its arrival.

Due to the continuing trend for desserts to be less substantial than the great variety of entrées and pièces de résistance that precede them, dessert knives and forks have gradually become less bold and bulky versions of their dinner namesakes. I am told by Mr. Owen that expediting this transition to the diminutive was the recognition that the acids in fruit could corrode steel, leading to the expensive silver-plating of dessert utensils. Smaller forks and knives meant significantly reduced costs. With time, service *à la russe* has extended throughout the length of a meal in order to include the expanding number of dishes that now com-

prise the dessert course itself. Caramel
Pudding, Pears and Whipped Cream,
Cheese Ramequins, Cheese Straws, Ices,
Sweet Biscuits, Grapes and Pears, Chocolates, Dried Fruits and Walnuts — each
dish is now served in sequential isolation
with its requisite cutlery.[31]

For some time, fruit pastry has also
appeared as a distinct dessert course, initially served with both a dessert fork and
knife. With its recent culinary transformation into a more delicate confection,
however, the pastry's soft texture can now
be cut by the downward thrust of the
dessert fork alone. As a result, it is no
longer customary to provide a knife when
fruit pastry is served.

Yet dessert forks were not intended to
be cutting utensils. This additional function placed inordinate stress on the lowest tine and many of these bent, rendering
the entire instrument useless. Given that
there is a subtle natural variation that occurs in tine widths under normal conditions (a point not previously appreciated
— see Note below), the dessert forks with
narrower lowest tine widths were gradu-

31. For a similar list of desserts, see the menu card preserved by Louis Ainsley, Figure 8.

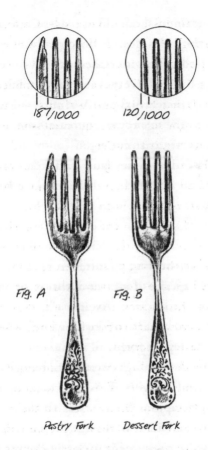

187/1000   120/1000

Fig. A   Fig. B

Pastry Fork   Dessert Fork

Figure 16. A Pastry Fork and Dessert Fork
(Illustrations by Thomas Darwin,
from "On the Effects of the Increased Use
of a Character in a Domestic Eating Utensil," 1879.)

ally extinguished. Those dessert forks with the widest lowest tine, by advantage, survived. Their increased use led to further gains in lowest tine width, much as exercise increases the bulk of one's muscle. Due to the agency of increased use, the lowest tine expanded significantly and the pastry fork — a new and distinctive variety of the dessert fork — has evolved into being.

Note
Using a dissecting microscope, I have conducted a series of measurements in twenty different locations (five per tine) on the width and breadth of the four tines of 144 unused dessert forks, all manufactured in 1870 as the Vintage pattern of silver plate, by Joseph Rogers & Sons, Ltd., an extremely reputable firm. For the sake of brevity, I will report only the measurements, in a single location, on the vertically lowest tine (with vertically lowest defined by right-handed use), though like variable findings were present at all locations (Fig. B).

When placed under the microscope, the width of the first lowest tine measured $120/1000$ of an inch in diameter when taken

½ of an inch from the tip. Measurements in the identical location on the remaining 143 forks were clustered, but not tightly, around this original measure, with a symmetrical distribution above and below the densest cluster at $125/1000$ of an inch. No two forks could be considered identical once measurements in ten different locations were considered.

As a point of comparison, the pastry fork depicted in Fig. A measures $187/1000$ of an inch at the location under discussion.

Shortly after the November reading, it occurred to Thomas, perhaps inspired by his intimate knowledge of his father's botanical experiments, that his conjecture concerning the origin of the pastry fork could be empirically established. Thomas undertook this challenge seriously. Throughout the remainder of his second year at Cambridge, he consumed fruit pastry for dessert at the conclusion of each evening meal, using the same dessert fork. He then faithfully recorded a measurement of its lowest tine width prior to retiring each night, no doubt hoping to document a gradual expansion.

Although never published, his experiment was presented as an oral paper to the *Plinian Society*. Its reception is recorded in the *Society*'s "minute-book" records of April 19th, 1879, as follows:

"Further to a previous presentation, Mr. Thomas Darwin communicated to the Society his series of measurements concerning the lowest tine width of a singular dessert fork, nightly challenged these past five months with the task of cutting and carrying fruit pastry from the plate to Mr. Darwin's mouth as a single utensil. No clear trend was discernible in his measurements, although a number of outlying findings prompted Mr. Venn to query whether the fork had been sufficiently cleaned on these occasions. Mr. Healey, left-handed, wished to know whether Mr. Darwin had encountered any pastry forks in which the upper tine was the widest and faced the 'wrong way' — 'not as yet,' replied Mr. Darwin. Mr. Ainsley congratulated Mr. Darwin on his experimental approach, and for his judicious choice of single subject methodology. All hailed Mr. Darwin's dexterity and a discussion of various pastry recipes then followed, after which the Society adjourned."

Although the above record implies that Thomas's ambiguous findings found a cordial reception, a careful reading of Ainsley's memoir suggests otherwise. In the week following Thomas's presentation, the Christ's College kitchen was broken into on three occasions. Though nothing obvious was stolen, drawers and cupboards were upended and their contents emptied. Ainsley suspected Thomas might have been responsible:

> "The kitchen was again found in disarray this morning. Most view the disturbance as a prank, suspecting the unpopular Mr. S—— from Trinity. But I confess I wonder about Thomas — no doubt still reeling from last week's brouhaha at the Society over his magically expanding fork fiasco. He appeared so sheepish this morning as we assisted the apologetic porters in righting the tables, rescuing all manner of entangled cutlery strewn upon the kitchen floor. At least tea was not delayed."

More amused than alarmed, Ainsley never communicated his suspicion to authorities.

Remarkably, Thomas Darwin's notions of artefact evolution continued to overlook the role of human agency. This omission, only subtly discernible in his account of the pastry fork, becomes very apparent when Thomas turns his attention to artefact "reproduction." Three curious items that had also been procured during his trip to Sheffield prompted this new area of interest. Once again, hand-drawn illustrations accompanied the article he submitted, this time to *Nature* just prior to the end of his second year at Cambridge.

EIGHT

Hybrid Artefacts

Cambridge, 10th May [1879]
To the Editor of Nature

Dear Sir,

I would be grateful if you would consider the enclosed manuscript for publication. The three illustrations serve as essential ancillary material. Fig. A is an olive spoon; Fig. B is a ramekin fork; and Fig. C is an oyster fork-spoon. I apologize for the salacious nature of the latter but this rare depiction of mechanical fusion in flagrante delicto warrants its inclusion, despite the explicit lewdness.

Respectfully submitted,

Thomas Darwin
Christ's College, Cambridge

Hybrid Artefacts and Their Role in Our Understanding of the Evolution of Inanimate Objects

In a brief report published earlier this year in the *Transactions of the Plinian Society*, vol. 9, pp. 19–22, I established that dessert forks of supposedly identical pattern could be distinguished from one another on a number of measurements. These random variations, which occur during production, whether by machine or by hand, account for an important source of novelty in the artefact world. It is their presence that represents the substrate for subsequent selection. Although the identical production of a given artefact (if it could be achieved) would immediately lead to a rapid increase in its numbers, this would represent only a temporary advantage. Ultimately, it is a variation that proves more adaptive and survives, the original artefact becoming extinct in due course.

I will now propose a far different mechanism for variation due to a process that I will term *spontaneous mechanical fusion*. It is not generally recognized that artefacts are capable of self-propagation.

However, in the process of spontaneous mechanical fusion, two distinct artefacts are, as it were, combined. The hybrid offspring of these spontaneous acts of fusion, I have come to realize, are the most important source of novelty in the artefact world. The mixing of the characteristics of both progenitors produces an abundant supply of variation in every generation. In what follows, I shall offer illustrative examples of hybrid products within the world of eating utensils. It will be understood that like argument is applicable to other artefact species and their varieties, although the high generality of the thesis remains to be empirically established.

The first specimen represented [Fig. A] is an olive spoon of the Vintage pattern of silver plate. The bowl of the olive spoon has two rudimentary tines, which spear the olive, and a large oval cutout, in which the olive is cradled, and through which residual liquid is drained. The mixing of characteristics of both its progenitors — a fork and spoon — can be easily appreciated.

The ramekin fork (or ramequin fork) [Fig. B] is a related hybrid. Although denoted a fork by most epicures, its four tines converge inwards from an enlarged common base to give an appearance more like that of a teaspoon. Its dual ancestry is also exposed by its narrowly separated tines which, towards their tips, are again joined across their width by a narrow span. Its unique structure is particularly adapted to custard and other congealed desserts, particularly if the targeted food is resident in small individual dishes.

Given their obvious dual characteristics, the olive spoon and ramekin fork each clearly represent a mature hybrid product of the fork and spoon species. The last example — the oyster fork-spoon [Fig. C] — differs in that it depicts the actual moment of an arrested coupling. As a result, it is particularly valuable in suggesting spontaneous mechanical fusion as the operative generative force as well as indicating the requisite anatomical positions for hybrid production. In this instance, it is as if a fork and spoon have been laid end-to-end and fused at their handles.

Despite the convincing evidence of the above examples, it is unclear whether all species and/or their varieties are capable of spontaneous mechanical fusion. To this end, and only after carefully scouring and drying all specimens, I have placed a

Fig. A   Fig. B   Fig. C

Figure 17. Hybrid Utensils: (left to right) Olive Spoon, Ramekin Fork, and Oyster Fork-Spoon. (Illustrations by Thomas Darwin, from "Hybrid Artefacts and Their Role in Our Understanding of the Evolution of Inanimate Objects," 1879.)

wide variety of forks and spoons in various positions of physical proximity. It seems to me worthwhile to give most of the experiments in detail.

First. — I laid the handle of a dessert fork end-to-end with the handle of a dessert spoon. After twenty-four hours, the two utensils could easily be separated. Microscopic inspection of the handles revealed no penetration. I repeated this experiment with the tines of the dessert fork now end-to-end with the bowl of the dessert spoon and in twenty-four hours attained similar negative results.

Secondly. — Repeated previous experiment, with the same results after seven days.

Thirdly. — I placed a dessert fork directly on top of a dessert spoon, with tines convex down. After twenty-four hours, the two utensils could be separated easily. There were no preliminary signs of penetration. I likewise tried the converse experiment, and placed a dessert spoon on top of a dessert fork, and in twenty-four hours attained similar negative results.

Fourthly. — Repeated previous experiment, with the same results after seven days.

Fifthly–Twenty-thirdly. — Experiments 1 to 4 repeated in the same manner, substituting dessert forks and spoons for the following varieties: dinner (four sizes), fish, lobster, crab, shrimp, berry, lettuce, terrapin, salad, cold meat, cheese, fruit, pickle, mango, relish, ice-cream, and pastry. All attempts to achieve a singular hybrid product were unsuccessful.

In contemplating the experimental results, the absolute sterility was, in some ways, not unexpected — perhaps parallel to the well-known futility of efforts to breed many animals in captivity. Experiments may have to be undertaken under less artificial conditions. Alternatively, greater gestational periods may be required; different positions may be more productive; and not all specimens may be fertile. Despite the need for further experimentation, the naturally occurring presence of hybrid artefacts is irrefutable.

Acknowledgment: I thank Master Cutler Robert Owen, who aided in the acquisition of many of the referenced specimens.

Figure 18. Sir Joseph Norman Lockyer

The arrival of the manuscript posed a dilemma for the Editor at *Nature*, Joseph Norman Lockyer. By 1879, the forthright Lockyer[32] had already served ten years as *Nature*'s founding editor and was familiar with most of the relatively small number of families from which the scientific men of Victorian England were drawn. Charles Darwin, already a revered figure in the scientific community, had been a frequent and eclectic contributor to the journal's early volumes. Lockyer would have appreciated Thomas's parentage and, no doubt, would have wished to avoid any embarrassment to the Darwin family. Given that the manuscript's central thesis was so peculiar, Lockyer may have wondered whether the work was intended to be a son's satirical and sophomoric prank upon his father. Perhaps upon reviewing Thomas's earlier publications in the *Transactions of the Plinian Society*, Lockyer concluded that Thomas's undertaking was meant for serious consideration and he evaluated the submission accordingly.

Judged on scientific terms, the kindest critique of Thomas Darwin's manuscript would begin by acknowledging the two valid premises contained within its opening paragraph. First, novel artefacts (i.e., artefacts that differ from their predecessors) are inadvertently

---

32. In reviewing one plan to construct a bridge across the English Channel, Lockyer wrote, "Our asylums produce innumerable schemes of this kind, but they are not permitted to disturb the public mind." (*Nature*, Dec 9, 1869)

produced during the process of mass production. Secondly, as only a small percentage of novel artefacts are ever integrated into the material culture of a society, competing artefacts are subjected to a selection process. Where Thomas became hopelessly muddled, however, was in his attempt to outline a previously unappreciated source of artefact novelty. As expressed in his words, "I will now propose a far different mechanism of variation which I will call *spontaneous mechanical fusion*." Thomas's conjecture was literal. In his mind, artefacts were not sterile physical objects. Instead, they were fertile entities capable of independent and spontaneous reproduction. Inexplicably, Thomas had overlooked the role that man played in overseeing and controlling the manufacture of artefacts in his "fusion" speculations.

One possible explanation for Thomas's confusion was the influence of Samuel Butler's *Erewhon*, a work published in 1872 and obviously familiar to Thomas, given the example of the tobacco pipe he borrowed from its pages. In *Erewhon*, Butler applied the idea of Darwinian evolution to the world of machines. Machines were evolving towards the capacity for reproduction, he argued, provided one was willing to extend the definition of what a reproductive system encompassed. To Butler, it included "machines which reproduce machinery." As an example, the thimble had a reproductive system, but this was the machinery that made it. Reluctantly, Butler still

Figure 19. Mr. Samuel Butler

included man in the process of mechanical reproduction, albeit in a maintenance role and with the
fearful anticipation that mankind's servitude to machines could only increase.

Thomas failed to grasp the satirical intent of
Erewhon. Perhaps encouraged by his father's earlier
exhortation, found in *On the Origin of Species*, "He
who will go thus far, ought not to hesitate to go one
step further," Thomas extended Butler's speculations
one literal step further. In Thomas's world, artefacts
no longer required man as the controlling agent
through whom reproduction occurred. If man had
any role at all, it was only as an unwitting voyeur.

Poor Lockyer. "Hybrid Artefacts and Their
Role in Our Understanding of the Evolution of
Inanimate Objects" was unpublishable, either as
satire or intended science. Fearing the latter, Lockyer
contacted Thomas's father.

London, 20th May [1879]

My dear Darwin,
   I have recently received a manuscript for
our journal's consideration from your son
Thomas. It is entitled "Hybrid Artefacts and
Their Role in Our Understanding of the
Evolution of Inanimate Objects." Although
it contains a number of valid observations,
I am seriously concerned that the majority

of its content reflects the reasoning of an unsound mind. I say this most respectfully and seek your counsel. Thomas, anxious about the priority of his findings, has already enquired as to the status of his submission. If his health is not well, I do not wish to exacerbate what may be a fragile state.

I look forward to your reply.

Sincerely,

Joseph Norman Lockyer

Charles Darwin's response was immediate.

Down, 23rd May [1879]

My dear Lockyer,

Thank-you for your letter of 20th May, 1879. I'm aware of and appreciate the courtesy you are extending to both Thomas and myself. For some time, my son has been excited about applying the arguments contained in On the Origin of Species to the world of man-made objects. Although I have not seen the recent submission to your journal, I am familiar with Thomas's work as reflected in the Transactions of the Plinian Society as well as the current direction of his academic interests.

In brief, I share your concern. Although I felt Thomas's earlier conjectures were insightful, his recent analogies and conclusions baffle me. I too have been at a loss as to how to gently convey my discomfort without stifling his enthusiasm or aggravating what I also see as a precarious mental condition. I can only add that Mrs. Darwin and I have privately urged Thomas to seek medical counsel. Thus far he refuses. Given our growing unease with Thomas's health, Mrs. Darwin intends to travel to Cambridge shortly to visit Thomas and assist as he allows.

In the interim, I'm afraid I must defer to your judgment on how best to deal with Thomas's submission. In no way do I question your estimation of my son's effort. But whether it is wise to be forthright with Thomas I cannot say. A father's grief clouds my objectivity.

Respectfully,

Charles Darwin

Ironically, had Charles Darwin read Thomas's manuscript, his estimations of the work may have been more favourable. In the early 1860s, Charles had conducted numerous fertility experiments with the various forms of two flowering plants: the crimson *Linum grandiflorum* and *Lythrum salicaria* (otherwise known as crimson flax and purple loosestrife, respectively). Charles had placed pollen from various-sized stamens of these plants onto the stigma of various-sized pistils and then, after different intervals, measured the penetration of the resulting pollen-tubes and/or seeds per capsule. There were endless permutations and repetitions to these meticulous experiments and the related publications were replete with sexual terms such as *hermaphrodite, male and female organs, penetration, fertility, castrated,* and *self-fertilization* as well as *legitimate, illegitimate,* and *artificial unions.*

Unaware that he may have inspired his son's methodology in "Hybrid Artefacts," Charles was as perplexed as Lockyer by Thomas's avenue of academic enquiry. In the absence of clear advice to the contrary, Lockyer sent Thomas the following succinct but candid letter.

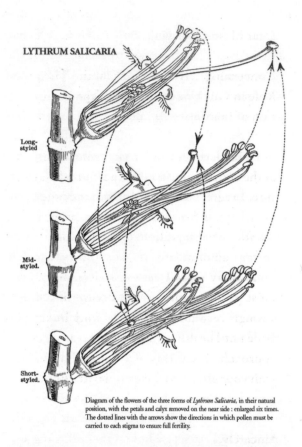

LYTHRUM SALICARIA

Long-styled

Mid-styled.

Short-styled.

Diagram of the flowers of the three forms of *Lythrum Salicaria*, in their natural position, with the petals and calyx removed on the near side : enlarged six times. The dotted lines with the arrows show the directions in which pollen must be carried to each stigma to ensure full fertility.

Figure 20. Three Forms of Lythrum Salicaria. From Darwin, C. *The Different Forms of Flowers on Plants of the Same Species*. London: John Murray, 1877.

London, 1st June [1879]

Dear Master Darwin,

Concerning "Hybrid Artefacts and Their Role in Our Understanding of the Evolution of Inanimate Objects."

Thank you for your recent submission of the above manuscript to the journal Nature. I regret to inform you that it cannot be accepted for publication. In brief, a number of observations, which display a certain amount of scientific ability, are undone by what I can only describe as most peculiar and unsound reasoning. I strongly recommend that this work be set aside until health permits a more reasoned approach. I say this after consultation with your esteemed father and with the utmost respect.

Sincerely,

Joseph Norman Lockyer

Lockyer's reference to Thomas's father was unfortunate. It suggested that Charles Darwin was also of the opinion that Thomas's reasoning was "most peculiar and unsound." Although a correct inference, it was far more blunt an assessment than Charles would have wished to convey to his son. Combined with the severity of Lockyer's critique, the belief that his own father was of similar mind must have represented a doubly harsh blow to Thomas.

The magnitude of the psychological impact of Lockyer's reply can only be judged by Thomas's subsequent actions. The letter of rejection from *Nature* would have arrived near the end of his second year at Cambridge. At summer break that year, Thomas uncharacteristically did not return to Down House. Instead, after meeting briefly with his mother in Cambridge, and without further communication with his father, he abruptly departed for North America.

PART THREE

ILLNESS

NINE

BUCKE — DARWIN LETTERS

On September 17th, 1879, after more than three anxious months without hearing from Thomas, a package arrived at the concerned Darwin household.[33]

23rd July [1879]

To Charles Darwin
Down, England

Dear Sir,
 It is with respectful trepidation that this letter is sent. I write from Canada as Medical Superintendent of the London (Ontario) Asylum for the Insane. Three

---

33. Although Charles Darwin made a general rule of keeping all correspondence that he received, the original letter from this package can not be located within the Darwin Archives. Fortunately, Dr. Bucke had his own general rule: the letters he sent were fair copies of drafts which he preserved. As such, the materials donated by the family of Dr. Bucke to the University of Western Ontario contained this draft of the letter Dr. Bucke wrote to Charles Darwin.

Figure 21. London Asylum.

weeks ago, a young man who gave his name as Thomas Darwin, age 21, was admitted by Lieutenant-Governor's Warrant to our institution. His birthplace was stated to be Down, England. Due to his diseased imagination, I have been cautious about my conclusions. However, the more coherent of his rambles leads me to this communication.

Without breaking the seal of my profession, I feel I can relay to you that the young man has the most intimate and plausible knowledge of the theory of natural selection. His intellectual life, including further details of his personal and family background, is otherwise difficult to access. Physically, he appears well — an asthenic build, approximately six feet in height and eleven stone in weight. A slight stoop but his gait is strong. I have taken the liberty of reviewing a biographical note that appeared in the Annals of the Royal Medical Society[34] — of eleven children, three deceased, your last was Thomas, born 1857. It is therefore with some confidence that this contact is made. I am now convinced Thomas is the most

---

34. In 1864, Charles Darwin was awarded the Copley Medal, the Royal Society's highest award.

immediate of your relations and that you would wish to know of his whereabouts and well-being. No family or friends have yet made enquiries and I fear he is alone on this continent.

In view of the delay between correspondences that an ocean imposes, I will proceed to a number of practical issues. Forgive this expedience, but I feel forthrightness is in Thomas's best interests. First, I wish you to be aware that our assistance is not intended to be aggressive. Thomas has received chloral hydrate for his rambles and poor sleep, but no other pharmaceuticals. Although viewed as dangerous prior to admission, he has not been violent and neither restraints nor seclusion have been required. As his health allows, we will encourage honest labour, fervent prayer, and his participation in constructive amusements. In time, recovery may follow. I would be pleased to keep you informed of his condition, and seek your own comments on any predisposing or exciting cause that may have contributed to Thomas's current admission. Specifically, if Thomas has intemperate habits, or has suffered accident, injury, or other adverse event, this information may prove helpful.

There is also the matter of upkeep. It is our policy to secure payments from all patients or their families except those in severe hardship. I trust the equivalent of $3.00 weekly (excluding the supply of clothing) will be viewed as reasonable, effective July 1879, and can be paid quarterly at your convenience — either to myself or directly to our bursar, Dr. Charles Sippi. I regret addressing this issue, particularly at this time, but our Inspector diligently monitors all such matters.

In closing, I would be remiss if I did not indicate my profound respect for your work and its influence on my recent publication, which I respectfully enclose. In different circumstances, I would be honoured to discuss my own unworthy vision of the universal harmony inherent in the evolutionary process. Should Thomas return to health, he would be most welcome to join the conversation.

Yours most sincerely,

Richard M. Bucke
Medical Superintendent
London Asylum

The publication Bucke enclosed was a copy of his recent book entitled *Man's Moral Nature* (New York: G. P. Putnam's & Sons). Published in 1879, sixteen copies of the 750 produced were sold during the book's first four years in print. With foresight, G. P. Putnam had agreed to accept the book provided costs of the print run were guaranteed by the author against future sales. In 1883, a resigned Bucke purchased all unsold copies (virtually the entire print run) from the publisher. At the time of his letter to Darwin, however, Bucke was still enthusiastically convinced that people all over North America were "anxious to buy it."

In *Man's Moral Nature*, Bucke offered a proof of moral evolution based on his detailed comparison of documents and artistic works of the nineteenth century to those he viewed as morally inferior from earlier times. Bucke's mechanism of explanation for man's "upward" moral evolution was based on Charles Darwin's theory of natural selection. Bucke argued that well-developed and superior morals aided survival or reproductive success. An individual with a well-developed sense of fear was more likely to live longer; an individual with a well-developed capacity for love was more likely to find a reproductive partner. As Bucke stated, such individuals who possessed an advanced moral nature, "must necessarily encroach upon the inferior individuals and races with whom they come into competition in the struggle for existence."

Given its obvious relation to Charles Darwin's interests, Bucke elected to forward a copy of *Man's Moral Nature* to Darwin along with his letter concerning Thomas. Even under the awkward circumstances, it was a remarkable demonstration of civility and restraint on Bucke's part not to explicitly seek comment about *Man's Moral Nature* from the great theorist himself. As Bucke later confided in his diary, however, "whatever Darwin thinks of it, good or bad, will be the measure of its Worth."

Despite Bucke's wish, Charles Darwin never read *Man's Moral Nature*. For many years, Darwin recorded the titles of "Books to Be Read" in a series of notebooks that are still preserved. In keeping with his relentless appetite to categorize, he listed scientific works on the left-hand pages of each notebook, non-scientific works on the right. Once read, the title of the book was entered again, this time in a "Books Read" section towards the back of the notebook and often with one or two summative notes. Charles Darwin must have skimmed *Man's Moral Nature* and gained a sense of its speculative nature, as the work was catalogued as non-scientific and listed amidst a number of novels and religious texts. Its title fails to appear again among the entries in the "Books Read" section.

Ironically, Bucke's notion that the forces of natural selection could operate on more than the physical characteristics of animals and plants was the same guiding principle that Thomas Darwin had imported into his own terrain of interest — in his case, not morals, but the world of inanimate objects. As Bucke learned more of his patient's beliefs, this coincidence would not escape him.

On October 11th, 1879, a letter from Down House finally arrived at the London Asylum.[35]

Down, 18th September [1879]

Dr. Richard M. Bucke
Medical Superintendent
London Asylum

Dear Doctor Bucke,
Thank you for your letter dated 23rd July 1879, which arrived in yesterday's post. The long delay may have been partly due to the kind enclosure (your book, which required inspection and clearance at the Post Office in London). In due course, I hope to review this impressive work. You will understand, however, that

35. The exchange between Bucke and Charles Darwin occurred by post. The telegraph was precluded due to each correspondent's decision to wed his letter to an enclosure (i.e., a book and cheque, respectively). It was not until the following year that "Professor Bell's new instrument" was introduced to the London Asylum. Shortt, *Victorian Lunacy*. Cambridge: Cambridge University Press, 1986, p 28.

my immediate concern is for dear Thomas, who is indeed our cherished youngest son. Our family has been extremely worried about his whereabouts since he departed from England earlier this year.

As Thomas has apparently been unable to speak for himself, Mrs. Darwin and I would be pleased to provide you with details of his health. Until the past year, this has been entirely unremarkable. Thomas was a healthy child, robust and well-behaved. We can recall only an infant's coughs and colds. There assuredly has been no vice or excess. Even as a young boy, Thomas had a serious and studious temperament — forever collecting this or that. An independent child, he needed encouragement to leave his hobbies or his books to join older siblings in play.

Approximately one year ago, our son's health began to change. Thomas became extremely preoccupied with the categorization and changing nature of artefacts or, as he would sometimes call them, "my" inanimate objects. Nothing else seemed to matter — including his formal studies, his social relations, and, alas, even his personal grooming. Yet he seemed to be on a legitimate voyage of discovery and, sympathetic to such journeys, I encouraged his enquiries. I now fear I was too supportive and seriously erred in not seeking help on his behalf. Perhaps he would have been more receptive to intervention at an earlier stage of his illness.

Strangely, I now find it hard to articulate precisely our initial concerns. As Thomas was away at Cambridge, our time together was limited. Yet this past Christmas — sadly, my own last contact with Thomas — not even well-meaning parents could overlook the obvious and disturbing changes that were present. I politely suggest that it is not only within your noble calling that illogical beliefs are combatted and conquered. But what Thomas began to exhibit was something far more than the unsound reasoning that frequently impedes a scientific enquiry. He developed a number of strange and unreasonable convictions, which persisted despite all evidence to the contrary. His diet became absolutely repetitive and rigid — pastry, of all foods! And he showed little interest in participating in the holiday celebrations.

Most hurtful, Thomas began to doubt my good intentions. Some time earlier, I had gently raised the importance of acknowledging those authors upon whom one's own work is based. Thereafter, Thomas seemed preoccupied with ensuring credit for virtually any observation he made. He became guarded and suspicious and no longer sought my advice or shared his manuscripts with me.

To our knowledge, throughout this past year, Thomas was never violent or despondent. I can recall observing only brief periods of agitation, and only when he was challenged on his beliefs. It is, therefore, with some incredulity we learn of his perceived dangerousness — his mother wishes me to emphasize his gentle nature.

We, of course, encouraged medical counsel as forcefully as parents could, but Thomas refused. At one point, I went so far as to feign an exacerbation of my own ailments in the hope that Thomas would join me at a water-cure establishment. To my disappointment, he was unreceptive. I am reasonably certain that Thomas has received no assistance prior to your care.

As to possible causes of Thomas's deterioration, I feel ill-equipped to comment. To my knowledge, there has been no recent accident. I emphasize, however, that we have had no contact with Thomas since he and Mrs. Darwin met in Cambridge on the morning of June 9th earlier this year. It was only then Thomas evasively informed his mother he planned to depart immediately for Canada. Our enquiries have led us to understand that one day later, Thomas left Cambridge for Liverpool and boarded the Canada-bound Peruvian. We have contacted the passenger line and Thomas's arrival in Quebec on June 18th has been confirmed. We were also informed that Thomas had purchased a ticket valid on the Grand Trunk Railway — destination uncertain. Beyond that, we are at a loss to comprehend what precisely motivated his journey or by what means he arrived at your facility — your letter is our first indication that Thomas has ventured in your direction.

Perhaps a precipitant to his current condition was rejection — a manuscript he recently submitted to the journal Nature was considered most unsound. From the concerns of the Editor, it seems to have been a tangled and unusual affair that, if published, would have reflected poorly on his abilities. According to Mrs. Darwin, Thomas took its refusal quite personally and somehow held me to blame. During their brief time together in Cambridge, he alluded to this matter — but only in vague and cryptic terms.

My wife also reports that during her brief visit in Cambridge, Thomas was even more preoccupied with artefacts than usual. Virtually his only conversation reiterated a need to study them in their wild state, in more primitive conditions. He mentioned Pitt Rivers and his work with Aboriginal weapons. In some way we believe this may be linked to the intent of his travels.

Aside from the above speculations, I can think of no other possible factors that may have contributed to Thomas's precarious state.

With respect to treatment, my wife is pleased to hear your mention of prayer and asks that you ensure Thomas attends Sunday service. We are relieved to learn that Thomas has not required restraints and trust that these will continue to be avoided.

We are, of course, extremely concerned about our son's condition and seek your counsel. Please be assured it is no reflection on the quality of the care that Thomas is currently receiving that we would prefer Thomas to be at home. If our son is well enough to travel, I would be indebted to you if his return to Down with an attendant could be immediately arranged. The cost of travel is of little concern and local treatment could be sought upon his arrival. If travel is precluded at this time, I intend to visit. Advice at your earliest convenience would be welcome.

In closing, my wife and I offer our sincere thanks for your kind involvement in Thomas's care. We now ask that you directly convey our love and concern to our son. A personal and private note to Thomas is enclosed.

Yours sincerely,

Charles Darwin

Post Script — As requested, a cheque for Thomas's upkeep at the Asylum is included.[36] Forgive me for hoping it far overestimates the length of Thomas's stay at your setting. Any excess funds may be used towards Thomas's escort home or the comfort of the other patients.

---

36. Fifty pounds according to an entry in Charles Darwin's 1879 ledger.

The most astonishing aspect of Charles Darwin's letter was his readiness to travel to Canada. By then, at age seventy, Charles was frail and essentially housebound; even local travel was an extreme exertion and avoided. Some years earlier, he could "hardly bear the fatigue" of attending his older daughter's wedding at a nearby village church. Still, Charles Darwin's resolve to be with Thomas was understandable. He and Emma had already experienced the loss of three children, one of whom, their ten-year-old daughter Annie, had died away from home. Shortly following her death, Charles privately recorded his and Emma's agony — "We have lost the joy of the household, and the solace of our old age. She must have known how we loved her. Oh, that she could know how deeply, how tenderly, we do still and shall ever love her dear joyous face! Blessings on her!"[37]

Charles and Emma's sentiments towards Thomas were equally profound. Their private note to Thomas, written by Charles, read as follows:

---

37. Annie Darwin died on April 23rd, 1851, during a visit to Dr. Gully's hydropathic establishment in Malvern after being unwell for almost one year. Charles Darwin was present but was too distraught to attend Annie's funeral. Emma had remained at home as she could not leave Down due to the late stage of her pregnancy with Horace. One week after Annie's death, Charles wrote an extremely moving and tender account of her chief characteristics; the quotation in the above text forms its last paragraph.

My dear Thomas,

We are all so relieved to learn of your whereabouts. Dr. Bucke has written to us of your illness, and I am confident you are in excellent medical hands. Your mother is extremely remorseful that she was unable to convince you to delay your trip. My own regret is learning of your departure only after it occurred — I feel very sorry not to have wished you well prior to your journey. I assure you I will make amends when we next embrace.

In the interim, your mother and I beseech you to focus all your energies on a return to health. When you are well, there will be more than enough time for scholarly enquiries. I too have experienced the frustration of lost days — but it is unwise to disregard the need for rest and treatment.

Everyone at Down House sends their love. We are all well, including your young nephew Bernard who wishes to report, "I are an extraordinary gooseberry-finder!" He misses you terribly and I sense he is anxious to be your assistant on your return. Polly, as well, suffers greatly. She keeps watch for you at the verandah window and is forever barking her disappointment at the arrival of less welcome guests.

Son, please be well and write when you are able. I have sought Dr. Bucke's permission for your return home. If for some reason this seems medically unwise, I am determined to visit.

Your Loving Father

Both Charles Darwin's letter to the doctor and his personal note to Thomas were tucked inside one of the diaries Bucke's family donated to the University of Western Ontario. Medical Superintendents then routinely opened letters written to and from patients and it was within their power to withhold all correspondence. Those letters deemed appropriate to deliver to patients were, once read by the intended recipients, retrieved and legally retained by the Asylum's Superintendent. The stated rationale of this highly restrictive administrative process was to protect patients from the potential ill-effects of their own mad ramblings. In fact, many of the letters to and from patients related to aggressive campaigns for release, and involved not just family members, but politicians, lawyers, police, and the press. As such, it was in the Administration's interest to be aware of such litigious crusades.

Thankfully, Bucke did choose to forward Charles Darwin's heartfelt letter to Thomas, albeit opened and obviously privy to its contents.

Unfortunately, based on a diary entry (see next Chapter), Thomas's physical health had deteriorated markedly by the time his father's letter arrived.

TEN

DR. BUCKE'S DIARY

Bucke's preserved diaries cover the period between 1877 and 1884. In general, he wrote brief notes every one to two weeks. In large part, entries were agonized, disjointed efforts to develop ambitious and coherent doctrines of mind, lunacy, and mental health. Specific references to patients were rare. Yet within a span of less than four months, Bucke made the following seven entries directly related to Thomas Darwin and his circumstances. Irrelevant intervening entries — largely concerning Bucke's disappointment with the reception and sales of *Man's Moral Nature* — have not been reproduced.

16th July, 1879

An intrigue. A fortnight ago, a new patient was admitted to the Asylum. He refuses — or is unable — to answer most questions. His documents list his name as Thomas Darwin, his home as Down, England — but I am not yet convinced that he is truly a relation of the eminent Charles

Darwin. Unlike his reticence to provide details of his personal life, the poor man rambles endlessly on about — of all things —
cutlery. A most unusual obsession.

28th July, 1879

Young Thomas continues unwell.
Chloral hydrate has had little effect and
sleep is minimal. I now lean towards believing he is indeed the son of Charles
Darwin and have written to the great man.
Brazenly, I enclosed a copy of Man's
Moral Nature with the correspondence.
Its review in AJI[38] has now been eagerly
forwarded by a number of ill-willed colleagues — "fanciful" methodology indeed.
Never mind — far more important —
whatever Darwin thinks of it, good or
bad, will be the measure of its Worth.

28th August, 1879

Young Thomas continues to occupy
my thoughts. I have transferred him from
the main building to one of the cottages.
He works well in the gardens and makes
good use of the library — reading aloud
to the illiterate. He has now read Man's

---

38. Review of *Man's Moral Nature* in "Book Notices." *American Journal of Insanity* 36, no. 4 (April 1880): 530-533.

Moral Nature and seems to have been unimpressed with its logic. Yet he read the book quickly — surely a positive sign.

At supper yesterday, an attendant confiscated a most peculiar utensil found beside his plate. I have it now before me — it is a singular object, as if a fork and spoon had been laid end-to-end and then fused at their handles. Its function, if any, is not obvious. Beecham is convinced it is an instrument for the pleasures of self-abuse. To appease him, I examined Thomas for flesh wounds but, thankfully, found none.

20th September, 1879

Still no word from Down. Thomas now tolerates my presence and we converse as my duties allow. He is a gentle soul but continues to be consumed with the strangest beliefs. He sees life in the man-made. Yet not all seems mad. I believe he views me as his student — yesterday I received a lecture on how the fork has evolved. Despite my efforts to maintain a professional stance, I was intrigued by the argument. Two prongs, to three, to four. In many ways, a scholarly account. And I, too, have seen the forces of selection where others have not.

12th October, 1879

Confirmation! Charles Darwin — the father — has written. A most respectful reply. I have conveyed to Thomas that his father and I have now corresponded and I delivered his father's note to him. For the first time, Thomas has requested pen and paper.

But his condition truly alarms me — now more physically than mentally. He is wasting and I fear has consumption. Sadly, despite his father's well-meaning enquiry, Thomas is too weak to travel.

Yet still Thomas lectures — other patients now attend to his observations. Even the violent gather quietly round as Thomas talks about the beauty in the man-made — how "endless forms most beautiful and most wonderful have been, and are being evolved."

In many ways, he has become a calming influence.

I have written Will to seek his assistance.

"Will" was a reference to Dr. William Osler, then working in Montreal and destined to become one of the preeminent physicians of the early twentieth century. In 1879, Bucke was reasonably good

Figure 22. Dr. William Osler

colleagues with Osler, despite the latter's younger age. The two physicians had met at a number of professional gatherings and discovered a shared love of literature, thereafter engaging in occasional correspondence. At Bucke's invitation, Osler had already visited the Asylum on more than a few occasions and had applauded Bucke on his efforts to eliminate restraints.

Both Bucke and Osler were actively involved with the Dominion Medical Association (the two served on a variety of committees, including joint membership on the Ethics Committee). Its twelfth annual session was to be held in London from October 16th to 18th and Bucke, as local host, was aware Osler would be attending as he was scheduled to give a number of anatomical demonstrations. Bucke also knew of Osler's interest in tuberculosis, particularly its pathology. As lecturer in the Institutes of Medicine at McGill, Osler had conducted numerous autopsies involving cases of tuberculosis, lecturing and publishing on his findings. He was also familiar with animal tuberculosis and the preliminary research suggesting that the disease could be transmitted to man from the infected meat and milk of animals. In an earlier visit to the London Asylum, Osler had cautioned Bucke about the importance of proper milk inspection as a preventative health measure.

From Bucke's next journal entry, it is apparent Osler graciously accepted Bucke's request to assess

Thomas during his visit to London. As Bucke feared, Osler confirmed the presence of a particularly malignant variant of tuberculosis in Thomas, and offered little hope for his recovery. Then known as the "typhoid" type, its rapidly progressive course was attributed to enormous numbers of the tubercle bacillus dispersed throughout the bloodstream. Thomas's advanced, incurable case left Osler with little to recommend but palliative measures and segregation from the other Asylum inmates.

20th October, 1879
Travel for Thomas is out of the question. Osler has confirmed a virulent and deadly strain of tuberculosis. The upper two-thirds of both lungs are actively involved. There is little to be done — comfort, God, and G.O.M.

"G.O.M.," or God's Own Medicine, was a reference to morphine. As for God, Bucke likely had a word with the Church of England clergy who conducted the service at the Asylum every Sunday. It was then customary to alert the relevant ministry that a patient's death was pending so that a prayer for the dying could be recited by the congregation.

23rd October, 1879

Our Thomas has died, a young gentleman of great name and of promise unfulfilled. I do not recall such anguish. He succumbed quickly to the tuberculosis. His last words — lucid and without embarrassment — "I forgive you."

I do not know how to convey such sorrow.

Oh Walt —

Come lovely and soothing death,
   Undulate round the world,
   serenely arriving, arriving,
In the day, in the night, to all, to each,
   Sooner or later, delicate death...[39]

Although the original London Asylum is no longer extant, the inscription "Thomas Darwin — Died 23rd October, 1879" is still visible on a small and weather-worn headstone in the original cemetery, now located on the grounds of the London Psychiatric Hospital.

Just prior to his death, Thomas wrote the following letter, never mailed, and found amongst the preserved correspondence of Dr. Bucke.

---

39. Bucke was quoting from Walt Whitman's "Death Carol." In *Leaves of Grass*, 38. New York: Smith & McDougal, 1872.

October, 1879

My dear Mother,

I have just read Father's letter. You must now know my whereabouts. Please do not feel badly or responsible — I thank you for tolerating my departure despite your deepest of reservations.

But now I must seek your help. I am here against my will in the most deplorable of situations. Arrest, warrant, and confinement — a conspiracy to declare me mad. <illegible> Bucke is the most villainous — two minutes a day at best with each inmate, then off to read Whitman. He now patronizes me to learn more of my scholarship. Yet he confiscates my specimens, their conjugal rights denied, whilst he ignores the assaults of his own staff. Mother — please God — you must obtain my release before harm comes.

As for F., please send my love and forgiveness. I could not have said good-bye. I continue my calling as best I can.

Your Loving Son,

Thomas

PART FOUR

EPILOGUE

ELEVEN

ONE STEP FURTHER

[It] is in line with the normal strategy of the natural
sciences to extend the use of ideas fruitful in one set of
inquiries into related domains.
— Nagel, E., 1966 [40]

Following publication of *On the Origin of Species*, it was
soon recognized that Charles Darwin's theories of evolution were applicable to subjects other than living organisms. Darwinian concepts quickly diffused into a
wide number of disciplines that included politics, literature, and sociology. The study of technology and its history also became heavily indebted to the work of Charles
Darwin. Analogies taken selectively from his theories of
organic evolution have helped shape our current understanding of technological innovation and artefact diversity. Today's experts on artefact evolution, able to
integrate the tenets of molecular genetics into their

---

40. Nagel, E. "The Meaning of Reduction in the Natural
Sciences." In *Science and Civilization*, edited by Robert C. Stauffer
and Richard Peter McKeon. Madison: University of Wisconsin
Press, 1966. p.124

analysis, speak of "striking parallels with genetic evolution... Innovations appear in the population in the manner of mutations, spread like genes, and are favoured or abandoned by processes resembling natural selection."

Yet before the widespread appreciation of Mendelian genetic principles, Thomas Darwin was already applying his father's concepts as explanatory devices for the diversity and evolution of artefacts. Thomas drew credible analogies between living organisms and material objects. In his published manuscripts, aside from his novel approach to the taxonomy of artefacts, he insightfully recognized competition between species as a causative agent for the formation of rudimentary characters. Of equal importance, due to an appetite for meticulous measurement, he identified the subtle variation of supposedly identical artefacts, even those which were mass-produced. This original and non-intuitive finding remains germane. Random variations still occur in manufactured artefacts "despite the rigid controls employed by modern industry", and with significant financial and legal repercussions.[41] Thomas was cor-

41. See Basalla, G. *The Evolution of Technology*, Cambridge History of Science Series. New York: Cambridge University Press, 1988. p.103. The many minor (and occasionally substantial) variations discernible in circulated coins invariably lead to collector items worth far beyond the face value of the coin. "Added value" also can occur from the successful lawsuits that anomalies of mass production can provoke, such as when an injury to a consumer results from a beverage can defect.

rect in asserting that these differences represented "the substrate for subsequent selection."

Thomas also recognized that one form of the inventive act can be viewed as "combining existing and known elements of culture in order to form a new element." Or, stated another way, Thomas recognized that the process of fusion was a blueprint for innovation. When features of A are fused with those of B, the novel product C emerges. Thus, when the fork and spoon are fused, it is the olive spoon, the ramekin fork, and the oyster fork-spoon that are generated — each new utensil highly advantaged in specialized circumstances. The explicit documentation of a formula for invention was a legitimate contribution by an early student of technological innovation, an area of study in which Thomas was a pioneer.

Until now, however, Thomas Darwin's legitimate insights as well as his interesting but flawed conjectures have been essentially unacknowledged and unknown. Given the exhaustive efforts to collate and record virtually all salient events of Charles Darwin's life, the current unfamiliarity with Thomas's academic undertakings, let alone the fact of his very existence, is baffling, particularly in view of the parallels between Charles's and Thomas's fields of enquiry.

The likely explanation for the intrigue now seems mundane — a proper Victorian family's inclination towards privacy. Charles and Emma Darwin were not inclined to reopen past sorrows for reasons of decorum and the magnitude of their own anguish. Following Annie's death, both found it too painful to speak publicly of their daughter again. With Thomas's death, it appears Charles and Emma again retreated into the silence of private grief.

Yet it remains unsettling that Emma's communication of Thomas's death within the Darwin family is incomplete and misleading — that is, that "Uncle Thomas died of tuberculosis while travelling in Canada." Again the explanation is likely banal. The stigma surrounding mental illness in Victorian England was profound and this surely contributed further to the anonymity of Thomas's life. Consistent with this thesis, Charles Darwin's failure to mention Thomas's striking family history of mental illness[42] when responding to Dr. Bucke's enquiry is also in keeping with the silencing power of stigma. Such concerns may also explain why Charles Darwin's autobiography and Emma Darwin's correspondence were so heavily edited by their surviving children prior to

42. At the time, Charles Darwin would have known that the symptoms of at least four family members were suspicious of mental illness: his maternal uncle, Tom Wedgwood, suffered recurrent depressions; a paternal uncle, Erasmus Darwin, Jr, drowned himself at age forty; his paternal half-cousin, Francis Galton, suffered a breakdown as a twenty-one-year-old student at Cambridge; and his older brother Erasmus was frequently in low spirits.

their publication. As Henrietta stated in the preface to the collection of her mother's letters, "I have, therefore, prepared them for publication by omitting what was of purely private interest." Perhaps letters concerning Thomas's mental illness were among those deemed too "private" to include.

As to the nature of Thomas's illness, the history of social isolation, odd behaviour, and subtle functional decline, followed by the onset of bizarre delusional beliefs is consistent with what would now be considered a major psychotic disorder. As discussed below, such a syndrome has complex and multiple causes, encompassing biological, psychological, and social considerations.

As formulated today, Thomas's biological risk of developing serious psychiatric illness would be significant based on the positive history of suicide, anxiety, and mood disorders within the extended Darwin family. Ironically, the one genetic factor that likely doesn't play a role is the one that most worried Charles and Emma — their marriage as first cousins.

Thomas's heightened vulnerability can also be attributed to his own unique psychological factors. Charles Darwin's role as the "invalid" within the family would predispose Thomas to a range of psychosomatic illnesses, as it did almost all Charles's other children. Further, Thomas's obvious personal and professional identification with his father may have placed him at greater (Oedipal) risk, especially if one views his field of chosen scholarship as a vehicle for competition.

There is a social context to consider as well. At the time of Thomas's "spontaneous fusion" conjecture, the scientific community was still seriously considering the possibility of spontaneous generation, whereby inanimate matter sprang into life. As an extension of this notion, Emma had once commented on her husband's unusual relationship with the sundew, the insectivorous plant (more properly referred to as *Drosera*) that Charles and Thomas together studied so closely: "At present he is treating *Drosera* just like a living creature, and I suppose he hopes to end in proving it to be an animal." Perhaps observing this aspect of his father's scientific method — his intense and complete immersion until all boundaries blurred — may be linked to Thomas's subsequent difficulties in recognizing the boundaries of the inanimate world.

Despite the above analysis, Thomas's diagnosis and its underlying cause is still in imperfect "Abstract" form. It is for others to now raise additional clinical considerations and to further examine the life and works of Thomas Darwin. Amongst the many potential lines of enquiry, it is to be hoped that investigators will wish to examine the fragile threshold between Thomas's ingenious insights and his "one step further" into the nether world of unreason. As Bucke stated, "We are too apt to draw the

Figure 23. Charles Darwin

line broad and strong and simply take for granted that on the whole the sane man thinks and feels correctly, and that the insane man thinks and feels incorrectly." On this point, Bucke and Charles Darwin agreed. In 1838, Charles wrote, "My F. says there is perfect gradation between sound people and insane. — that everybody is insane, at some time."[43] Charles Darwin must often have pondered the fine line that separated his son's creative insights and his madness. And perhaps wondered whether, like Thomas, he, too, had teetered between the worlds of reason and unreason.

In the end, Charles Darwin lies buried in Westminster Abbey, his son Thomas on the grounds of the London Asylum.

One long argument. One step further.

---

43. F. refers to Charles's father, Dr. Robert Waring Darwin, a respected physician who believed he had a particular facility in recognizing the unexpressed emotional concerns of his many patients.

Thomas Darwin
A Brief Chronology

1808, May 2	Birth of Emma Wedgwood
1809, February 12	Birth of Charles Darwin
1828 to 1831	Charles Darwin attends Cambridge University
1831, December 27 to 1836, October 2	Charles Darwin's five-year voyage aboard the *Beagle*
1839, January 29	Marriage of Charles Darwin and Emma Wedgwood
1839, December 27 to 1856, December 6	Births of William Erasmus, Anne Elizabeth, Mary Eleanor, Henrietta Emma, George Howard, Elizabeth, Francis, Leonard, Horace, and Charles Waring
1842, September 14	Emma and Charles Darwin move to Down House
1857, December 10	Birth of Thomas Darwin
1859	Charles Darwin publishes *On the Origin of Species by Means*

	of Natural Selection, or the Preservation of Favoured Races in the Struggle for Life
1868, autumn to 1877, spring	Thomas Darwin attends Clapham from the ages of ten to nineteen
1869	Thomas and Horace Darwin publish "Coinage of the Ancient Britons at Down"
1872	Charles Darwin publishes *The Expression of the Emotions in Man and Animals*
1872	Samuel Butler publishes *Erewhon, or Over the Range*
1877, autumn	Thomas Darwin begins studies at Cambridge
1878, summer	Thomas Darwin publishes "Artefacts and the Origin of Their Rudimentary Characters: By Means of Competition Between Species"
1878, August 2 to 5	Thomas Darwin visits Sheffield
1879, spring	Thomas Darwin publishes "On the Effects of the Increased Use of a Character in a Domestic Eating Utensil"
1879, spring	Dr. Richard Maurice Bucke publishes *Man's Moral Nature*

1879, May 10	Thomas Darwin submits "Hybrid Artefacts and Their Role in Our Understanding of the Evolution of Inanimate Objects" to the journal *Nature*
1879, June 1	"Hybrid Artefacts and Their Role in Our Understanding of the Evolution of Inanimate Objects" is rejected for publication
1879, June 11 to 18	Thomas Darwin travels from Liverpool to Quebec aboard the *Peruvian*
1879, June 20	Thomas Darwin arrested in Toronto, Ontario
1879, July 2	Thomas Darwin admitted to the London Asylum, Ontario
1879, October 23	Death of Thomas Darwin
1882, April 19	Death of Charles Darwin
1896, October 2	Death of Emma (Wedgwood) Darwin

Sources for Quotations

Preface

"scant though this admitting information was ..." (Shortt, S. E. D. *Victorian Lunacy: Richard M. Bucke and the Practice of Late Nineteenth-Century Psychiatry.* Cambridge History of Medicine Series. New York: Cambridge University Press, 1986, p.50.)

"dangerous to others" (see Chapter 4, p 84.)

"Death due to tuberculosis..." (RG 10-279. *London Asylum Patients' Clinical Casebooks, October 23, 1879.* Archives of Ontario. p.178.)

Chapter One – Down House

"My dearest Aunt Fanny..." (Emma Darwin to Fanny Allen, December 10th, 1858. In Darwin, Elizabeth. *My Dearest Aunt Fanny, My Dear Emma: The Correspondence of Mrs. Emma (Wedgwood) Darwin and Miss. Fanny Allen.* p.224.)

"with a sudden leap"; "pungent" ; "Tragically, your Uncle Thomas ..." (Emma Darwin to Gwen Raverat, August 16th, 1892. In Darwin, Elizabeth. *Dear Emma,* p.318.)

"very stout and nervous" (Raverat, Gwen. *Period Piece: A Cambridge Childhood*. London: Faber and Faber, 1952. p.146.)

"been an invalid all her life" (Ibid., p.121.)

"no spring of hope in him" (Ibid., p.191.)

"inherited the family hypochondria in a mild degree" (Ibid., p.196.)

"always retained traces of the invalid's outlook" (Ibid., p.204.)

"nerves always as taut as fiddle strings" (Ibid., p.187.)

"When there were colds about ..." (Ibid., p.123.)

"Do you think, Papa ..." (Emma Darwin to Fanny Allen, August 16th, 1866. In Darwin, E. *My Dearest Aunt Fanny*, p.301.)

"Alone, but not lonely." (Emma Darwin to Fanny Allen, May 23rd, 1861. Ibid., p.262.)

"never to beat Papa." (Emma Darwin to Fanny Allen, February 3rd, 1858. Ibid., p.212.)

"now bow your necks, and say 'quack.'" (Andersen, H. C. *Danish Fairy Legends and Tales*. London: William Pickering, 1846. p.32.)

"Now the tally with my wife ..." (Darwin, Emma Wedgwood. *Emma Darwin, a Century of Family Letters, 1792-1896*. Vol II. London: J. Murray, 1915. p.221.)

Chapter Two – School Days

"Thomas Darwin, son of Charles Darwin, of Down"; "country gentleman." (RG 14-307. *The*

General Admission Register of the Clapham School, September 14, 1868. National Archives of England. p.136.)

"June 1st, 1869. Thomas has passed the year's examinations ..." (RG 14-512. *Student Casebooks of the Clapham School*, June 1, 1869. National Archives of England. p.92.)

"June 3rd, 1872. Thomas is a quiet and ..." (RG 07-512. Ibid., June 1, 1872. p.93.)

"Still alone but not lonely." (Emma Darwin to Fanny Allen, March 4th, 1869. In Darwin, E. *My Dearest Aunt Fanny*, p.331.)

"The children are well ..." (Emma Darwin to Fanny Allen, April 13th, 1875. Ibid., p.441.)

"when properly excited," Darwin, Charles. *The Autobiography of Charles Darwin*. 1958, p. 50.

"As good as new!" (Emma Darwin to Fanny Allen, June 12th, 1874 Ibid., p.401.)

"his quiet cob Tommy stumbled and fell, rolling on him ..." Darwin, Emma. *Emma Darwin, a Century of Family Letters. Vol. II*, p. 195.)

"There is such a strong inclination ..." (Emma Darwin to Fanny Allen, July 15th, 1872. In Darwin, E. *My Dearest Aunt Fanny*. p.358.)

"Thomas, never having taken to dancing ..." (Emma Darwin to Fanny Allen, August 15th, 1872. Ibid., p.363.)

"companionship of clever men at clubs over female chit-chat in the drawing-room." (Emma Darwin to Fanny Allen, December 20th, 1874. Ibid., p.418.)

Chapter Three – Cambridge University

"I am well and now equally well settled ..." (see Chapter 5, p 107)

"At the insistence of the Society ..." (RG 14-473. *Minute-Book Records Plinian Society, November 17, 1877.* Archives of the University of Cambridge. p.280.)

"Perhaps the strangest member ..." (Ainsley, Louis. *Looking Back.* Printed for Private Circulation, 1930. p.89.)

Chapter Four – London Asylum

"That he is insane in the expression ..." (RG 10-268. Dr. M. Nichol, *London Asylum Admission Warrants and Histories, June 24, 1879.* Rare Book Room, University of Western Ontario.)

"His talk suggests mental delusions ..." (RG 10-284. Dr. R. H. Clark, Ibid.)

"At least throughout the last two days ..." (RG 10-149. Justice R. M. Stevenson. Schedule 2. Ibid. June 26, 1879.)

"of the life and order of the universe" (Bucke, Richard Maurice. *Cosmic Consciousness: A Study in the Evolution of the Human Mind.* Secaucus, N.J: Citadel Press, 1993. p.2.)

"The Victoria affair is hopefully behind us ..."
Langmuir J. W. to R. M. Bucke, October 17th,
1877. Rare Book Room at the University of
Western Ontario.

"was so intense and of such long standing ..." (Kaplan, Justin. *Walt Whitman, a Life*. New York:
Simon and Schuster, 1980. p.35.)

"silver wire" (Shortt, S. E. D. *Victorian Lunacy*, 1986,
p. 125.)

"villainous" (see Chapter 10, p 185)

"the very violent, the very dirty, ..." (Langmuir, J. W.
*Twelth Annual Report of the Inspector of
Asylums, Prisons and Public Charities for the
Province of Ontario, for the Year Ending 30th
September, 1879*. Toronto: C. Blackett Robinson, 1880. p. 329)

"a young gentleman of great name ..." (see Chapter
10, p. 184)

Chapter Five – Species and Varieties

"collection and observation ..." (Greenacre, Phyllis. *The
Quest for the Father: a Study of the Darwin-Butler
Controversy, as a Contribution to the Understanding of the Creative Individual.* New York: International Universities Press, 1963. p. 29.)

"many more individuals of each species ..." (Darwin,
Charles. *On the Origin of Species*, 1859. p. 5.)

"This preservation of favourable ..." (Darwin,
Charles. *The Origin of Species* 1876, p. 63.)

"one long argument" (Ibid., p. 404.)

"use in our domestic animals ..." (Ibid., p. 108.)

"success as a man of science" (Darwin, Charles. *The Autobiography of Charles Darwin*. 1958, p. 58.)

"an account of the development ..." (Ibid., p. 5.)

Chapter Six – Rudimentary Characters

"*Hat doch der Wallfisch* ..." (Barlow, Nora, ed. *The Autobiography of Charles Darwin, 1809-1882: With Original Omissions Restored*. London: Collins, 1958. p.211.)

Chapter Seven – The Pastry Fork

"Mr. Thomas Darwin communicated to the *Society* ..." (RG 14-471. *Minute-Book Records of the Plinian Society, October 28, 1878*. Archives of the University of Cambridge. p.313.)

"Further to a previous presentation ..." (RG 14-203. Ibid., April 23, 1879. p.341.)

"The kitchen was again found in disarray ..." (Ainsley, L. *Looking Back*, p.138.)

Chapter Eight – Hybrid Artefacts

"I will now propose a far different mechanism ..." (see Chapter 8, p. 140.)

"machines which reproduce machinery" (Butler, Samuel. *Erewhon, or Over the Range*. London: Penguin Books, 1985. p. 211.)

"He who will go thus far ..." (Darwin, Charles. *The Origin of Species*, 1876, p. 145.)

Chapter Nine – Bucke – Darwin Letters

"anxious to buy it" (Shortt, *Victorian Lunacy*, p.82.)

"must necessarily encroach upon ..." (Bucke, R. M. *Man's Moral Nature: An Essay*. Toronto: Willing and Williamson, 1879. p. 160.)

"whatever Darwin thinks of it ..." (see Chapter 10, p. 178)

"hardly bear the fatigue" (Darwin, Charles. *The Autobiography of Charles Darwin*, 1958, p. 85.)

"We have lost the joy of the household ..." (Darwin, Emma. *Emma Darwin, a Century of Family Letters. Vol II.*, p. 139.)

Chapter Ten – Dr. Bucke's Diary

"endless forms most beautiful ..." (Darwin, Charles. *The Origin of Species*, 1876. p. 429.)

Epilogue – One Step Further

"[It] is in line with the normal strategy ..." (Nagel, E. "The Meaning of Reduction in the Natural Sciences." In *Science and Civilization*, edited by Robert C. Stauffer and Richard Peter McKeon. Madison: University of Wisconsin Press, 1966. p. 124.)

"striking parallels with genetic evolution ..." (Lumsden, Charles J. and Edward O. Wilson. "The Relation between Biological and Cultural Evo-

lution." *Journal of Social and Biological Systems*
8, no.4 (1985). p. 350.)

"combining existing and known elements ..."
(Basalla, George. *The Evolution of Technology.*
Cambridge History of Science Series. New
York: Cambridge University Press, 1988. p.21.)

"Uncle Thomas died of tuberculosis ..." (see Chapter
1, p. 32)

"I have, therefore, prepared ..." (Darwin, Emma.
Emma Darwin, a Century of Family Letters. Vol
I. p.ix.)

"At present he is treating *Drosera* ... " (Darwin,
Emma. *Emma Darwin,* Vol II. p.177.)

"We are too apt to draw the line broad ..." (Bucke,
R. M. "Sanity." *American Journal of Insanity* 47,
no.1B (July 1890): p. 18.)

"My F. says ..." (Darwin, Charles. *Notebook M*:
[*Metaphysics on morals and speculations on
expression (1838)*]. CUL-DAR125. Transcribed
by Kees Rookmaaker. Darwin Online.
http://darwin-online.org.uk/ (accessed June 1,
2010).

Acknowledgments

"had been deeply impressed ..." (Darwin, Charles.
The Autobiography of Charles Darwin, 1958, p.
57.)

"I could produce variously coloured ..." (Ibid., p.6.)

Author's Notes
and Acknowledgments

The Evolution of Inanimate Objects: The Life and Collected Works of Thomas Darwin (1857-1879) is (emphatically!) a work of analogy and fiction. This open acknowledgment of the manufactured nature of this work distinguishes it from those rare publications which are presented as if true, and whose falsification remains concealed, a deceit seen in science as well as in art. With respect to the former, Charles Darwin recalled in his autobiography that he encountered only three intentionally falsified reports throughout a life in science. One was particularly impudent and involved a concocted communication in the *American Agricultural Journal* of a putative new breed of oxen. To Darwin's consternation, the rogue author included mention of their supposed correspondence; even going on to say that Darwin "had been deeply impressed with the importance of his result". Interestingly, Charles Darwin neglected to include a fourth incident in his tally. An eight-year-old Charles Darwin conveyed to a classmate that, "I could produce variously coloured polyanthuses and primroses by watering them with certain coloured fluids." By Charles Darwin's own admission this was, of course, an outrageous fable.

Thomas Darwin is a fictional character. It follows that the purported letters written to and by him, the manuscripts attributed to him, and the references to him within otherwise genuine works and correspondence have all been contrived, as has the apparent assistance of *Nature*'s head office. Although the manuscripts credited to Thomas Darwin were constructed, their content relies heavily upon two streams of legitimate scholarship: the publications of Charles Darwin, and their subsequent expert analysis; and two works concerning technological innovation, *The Evolution of Useful Things* by Henry Petroski and *The Evolution of Technology* by George Basalla, which together provided the paradigm of eating utensils and many of the details concerning organic-mechanical analogies. The content of Thomas's manuscript on "Artefacts and the Origin of Their Rudimentary Characters: By Means of Competition Between Species" draws heavily upon factual material in Petroski's chapter "How the fork got its tines." Although Petroski's paradigm is that form follows failure, the character of Thomas has chosen to emphasize the competition between species to account for the table knife's evolution in form. The story behind the pronounced cutting tine of the pastry fork is also recounted in

Petroski's book, in this case as a needed improvement on forks with thinner and weaker tines which bent on cutting. To my knowledge, Thomas's explanation of the enlarging tine's inheritance is a novel, albeit flawed insight, as is his notion of spontaneous mechanical fusion to account for hybrid objects.

Charles Darwin's *On the Origin of Species* also played a significant role in this account, not only for the content and terms it provided but also for establishing a literary tone worth emulating. Despite admonitions, Thomas was not always consistent in citing *On the Origin of Species* when quoting his father's work. A number of Charles Darwin's other works also provided important theoretical and stylistic templates: the observations of Thomas were inspired by *The Expression of the Emotions in Man and Animals* and "Biographical Sketch of an Infant", the latter reflecting Charles's observations of his infant son William; the experiments within the "Hybrid Artefacts" manuscript were based upon methodology Charles used to prove two forms of the *Linum grandiflorum* ["On the Existence of Two Forms, and on Their Reciprocal Sexual Relation, in Several Species of the Genus *Linum*." *Journal of the Proceedings of the Linnean Society (Botany)*, (1864) 7: 69–83.]; while the "Sheffield Notebook" includes phrases from the notes Charles made during an expedition to Northern Wales ("On the Ova of *Flustra*, or, Early Notebook, Containing Observations Made by C. D. When He Was at Edinburgh, March 1827." In *The Collected Papers of Charles Darwin*, edited by P. H. Barrett. Vol. 2, 285-291. Chicago: Chicago University Press, 1977.). Articles authored by his children also deserve mention. The wording used in *Coinage of the Ancient Britons at Down* incorporates text from a notice Francis, Leonard, and Horace Darwin submitted to the *Entomologist's Weekly Intelligencer* concerning three unusual beetles captured close to Down. As for George Darwin's calculations related to first cousin marriages, further details can be found in his 1875 paper titled "Marriages Between First Cousins in England and Their Effects."

The circumstances of the Darwin family integrated into the fabric of Thomas Darwin's life draws upon the correspondence to and from Emma and Charles Darwin, particularly as found within Emma's collection of family letters edited by her daughter Henrietta, and the definitive and exhaustive collections of Charles Darwin's correspondence published by Cambridge University Press and now available online. Other helpful sources included Charles Darwin's autobiography, various essays by his son Francis, Gwen Raverat's memoir *Period Piece* (whose contents provided such details as Henrietta's "stinkhorn" game, the menu for Ainsley's "Grand Dinner" and a comment reassigned to Emma on the predilection of the Darwins and Wedgewoods to marry first cousins), an article published by the numismatist Sir John Evans in *Notices and Proceedings of the Royal Institution of Great Britain*, and a number of biographies of Charles Darwin, particularly A. Desmond and J. Moore's *Darwin: The Life of a Tormented Evolutionist*. As for the portrayal of the London Asylum and its Medical Superintendent, Richard M. Bucke, the principal reference consulted was S. E. D. Shortt's insightful book, *Victorian Lunacy: Richard M. Bucke and the Practice of Late Nineteenth-Century Psychiatry*. It was Shortt, for example, who originally articulated *Man's Moral Nature* as Bucke's vision "of the universal harmony inherent in the evolutionary process." (*Victorian Lunacy*, p. 91). The juxtaposition of the Bucke-Whitman photos used in Chapter 4 is identical to Phillip Leon's creative selection and juxtaposition of the same two photos in his book *Walt Whitman & Sir William Osler: Poet and Physician*. The 1879 and 1880 annual reports of Ontario's Inspector of Asylums, Prisons, and Public Charities also contributed important material to the characterization of Bucke and his activities.

The many other scholars whose works helped shape Thomas Darwin's life are acknowledged by their presence in the bibliography. At times, dates of events have been changed; the experiences of others have been reassigned to Thomas; genuine quotations have been altered as in such aberrations as "Do you think, Papa ..." and "I are an extraordinary gooseberry-finder!"; and direct quotes, and near-quotes, have been integrated into the text, as in Emma's letter to Aunt Fanny, Thomas's soundless speech, the "Sheffield Notebook" and Thomas's various ruminations on the rudimentary regression of coins. The following sources have been invented altogether: *The Oxbridge Unabridged Correspondence of Charles Darwin: The Standard Reference*; *My Dearest Aunt Fanny, My Dear Emma: The Correspondence of Mrs. Emma (Wedgwood) Darwin and Miss Fanny Allen Darwin*; *London Numismatics Monthly Intelligencer*; *Dear Emma*; and *Looking Back*.

Thank you to those who kindly granted permission to reproduce the photographs within this work or assisted with their acquisition: John Lutman and Barry Arnott, The University of Western Ontario; Adam Perkins, Ruth Long, and Don Manning, Cambridge University Library; Kathryn McKee, St John's College, Cambridge; Gerald White, Norman Lockyer Observatory, England; Cathy Wright, Pitt Rivers Museum, Oxford; Lily Szczygiel, Pamela Miller and Christopher Lyons, Osler Library of the History of Medicine, McGill University; and Steven Birks, North Staffordshire Potteries website. The lines from "pity this busy monster, manunkind," are used by permission of Liveright Publishing Corporation. Special thanks to Catherine MacDonald whose drawings, including those misattributed to

Thomas Darwin, are an essential contribution to this book's character.

Thank you to those individuals and institutions who kindly aided the progression of this work: the archivist John Court, Centre for Addiction and Mental Health (CAMH), Toronto; Christine Adams, Scott Anderson, Ben Hart, Karen MacDonell, and their colleagues at the College of Physicians and Surgeons of British Columbia Library; Dr. Sam Sussman, London Psychiatric Hospital; the Archives of Ontario; Gillian Rodgerson, Insomniac Press; Corinna Harrod, Harper-Collins UK; Kim Sparks, Heather MacDonald, Michelle Purcell, Andrea Freeman, and Jane Sayers. This work was also supported by a Hewton Bursary awarded by the Friends of the Archives at CAMH, Toronto.

Thank you to my fellow writers in the fiction stream of Simon Fraser University's Writer's Studio, class of 2009 — Robin Evans, Berenice Freedome, Helen Heffernan, Anne Hopkinson, Antonia Levi, Fainne Martin, and Caroline Purchase; to Elizabeth, April, and Franny Karlinsky for their page-by-page scouring of the "minute-book" records of the *Plinian Society*, *Nature*, and other potential sources of previously unappreciated or unrecognized material related to Thomas Darwin; and to Sally Karlinsky, Guy Kay, Joe Berg, Anne Lennox, my sisters Karen, Ellen, and Amy, and to my parents Minnie and William Karlinsky for their unwavering encouragement and support.

The various editions of this novel would not have been possible without the enthusiasm and support of Carolyn Swayze and Kris Rothstein of Caroline Swayze Literary Agency Ltd, Mike O'Connor, publisher of Insomniac Press, and Scott Pack, the Publisher of the HarperCollins UK, The Friday Project imprint.

Finally, special thanks to my editor Anne Stone.

BIBLIOGRAPHY

Allan Line. *Illustrated Tourists' Guide to Canada and the United States*. Liverpool: Turner & Dunnett, 1880. http://www.archive.org/ stream/cihm_ 06450#page/n5/mode/2up (accessed June 15, 2010). Also available in print form and microfiche.

Alvarez, W. C. "The Nature of Charles Darwin's Lifelong Ill-Health." *The New England Journal of Medicine* 261 (Nov 26, 1959): 1109-1112.

Andersen H. C. *Danish Fairy Legends and Tales* [Translated by Caroline Peachey]. London: William Pickering, 1846.

Atkins H. *Down: The Home of the Darwins*. London: Royal College of Surgeons of England, 1974.

Barfoot, M. and A. W. Beveridge. "Madness at the Crossroads: John Home's Letters from the Royal Edinburgh Asylum, 1886-87." *Psychological Medicine* 20, no. 2 (May, 1990): 263-284.

Barlow, Nora, ed. *The Autobiography of Charles Darwin, 1809-1882: With Original Omissions Restored*. London: Collins, 1958.

Barrett, Paul H. *The Collected Papers of Charles Darwin*. Chicago: University of Chicago Press, 1977.

Basalla, George. *The Evolution of Technology*. Cambridge History of Science Series. New York: Cambridge University Press, 1988.

Bateson, Dusha and Jarieway, Weslie. *Mrs Charles Darwin's Recipe Book: Revived and Illustrated*. New York: Glitterati Inc. 2008.

Bowlby, John. *Charles Darwin: A Biography*. London: Hutchinson, 1990.

Brock, Patrick W. and Basil Greenhill. *Steam and Sail: In Britain and North America; 80 Photographs Mainly from the National Maritime Museum Depicting British and North American Naval, Merchant and Special Purpose Vessels of the Period of Transition from Sail to Steam*. Princeton, N. J.: Pyne Press, 1973.

Bucke, Richard Maurice. *Cosmic Consciousness: A Study in the Evolution of the Human Mind*. Secaucus, N. J.: Citadel Press, 1993.

———. *Man's Moral Nature: An Essay*. Toronto: Willing and Williamson, 1879.

———. "Sanity." *American Journal of Insanity* 47, no.1B (July 1890): 17-26.

———. "The Origin of Insanity." *American Journal of Insanity* 49, no.1 (July 1892): 56-66.

Burkhardt, Frederick and Sydney Smith, eds. *The Correspondence of Charles Darwin*. 18 vols.:

1821-1870. New York: Cambridge University Press, 1985-2010.

Burton, Elizabeth. *The Pageant of Early Victorian England, 1837-1861.* New York: Scribner, 1972.

Butler, Samuel. *Erewhon, or Over the Range.* London: Trübner and Co., 1872.

———. *Erewhon, or Over the Range.* London: Penguin Books, 1985.

———. *The Family Letters of Samuel Butler, 1841-1886* [Edited by Arnold Jacques Silver]. London: Jonathan Cape, 1962.

Clark, Ronald W. *The Survival of Charles Darwin: A Biography of a Man and an Idea.* New York: Random House, 1984.

Colp, Ralph, Jr. "Notes on Charles Darwin's 'Autobiography.'" *Journal of the History of Biology* 18, no. 3 (Autumn, 1985): 357-401.

———. *To be an Invalid: The Illness of Charles Darwin.* Chicago: University of Chicago Press, 1977.

Cummings, E. E. *Complete Poems, 1904-1962.* [Edited by George James Firmage]. New York: Liveright, 1991.

Darwin, Charles. "A Biographical Sketch of an Infant." *Mind: Quarterly Review of Psychology and Philosophy* 2, no. 7 (1877): 285-294.

———. *Insectivorous Plants.* London: J. Murray, 1875.

————. *Notebook M*: [*Metaphysics on morals and speculations on expression* (1838)]. CUL location-DAR125. [Transcribed by Kees Rookmaaker] Darwin Online. http://darwin-online.org.uk/ (accessed June 1, 2010).

————. "On the Existence of Two Forms, and on Their Reciprocal Sexual Relation, in Several Species of the Genus Linum." *Journal of the Proceedings of the Linnean Society (Botany)* 7 (1863): 69-83.

————. *On the Origin of Species by Means of Natural Selection: Or, the Preservation of Favoured Races in the Struggle for Life*, 1st ed. London: J. Murray, 1859.

————. "On the Ova of *Flustra*, Or, Early Notebook, Containing Observations Made by C. D. When He was at Edinburgh, March 1827." In *The Collected Papers of Charles Darwin*, edited by P. H. Barrett. Vol. 2. Chicago: Chicago University Press, 1977. pp. 285-291.

————. "On the Sexual Relations of the Three Forms of Lythrum Salicaria." *Journal of the Linnean Society of London (Botany)* 8, no. 31 (1864): 169-196.

————. "Preliminary Notice." In *Erasmus Darwin*, by Ernst Krause, 1. [Translated from the German by W. S. Dallas]. London: J. Murray, 1879.

————. *The Autobiography of Charles Darwin, and Selected Letters* [Edited by Francis Darwin]. New York: Dover Publications, 1958.

———. *The Descent of Man, and Selection in Relation to Sex*. Princeton, N. J.: Princeton University Press, 1981.

———. *The Expression of the Emotions in Man and Animals*. 1st ed. London: J. Murray, 1872.

———. *The Expression of the Emotions in Man and Animals / Essay on the History of the Illustrations by Phillip Prodger* [Edited by Phillip Prodger and Paul Ekman]. London: Harper Collins, 1998.

———. *The Formation of Vegetable Mould, Through the Action of Worms, with Observations on Their Habits*. London: J. Murray, 1881.

———. *The Origin of Species by Means of Natural Selection: Or, the Preservation of Favoured Races in the Struggle for Life*, 6th ed. London: J. Murray, 1876.

———. *The Variation of Animals and Plants Under Domestication*. 2 vols. 1st ed. London: J. Murray, 1868.

Darwin, Charles and Alfred Russel Wallace. "Three Papers on the Tendency of Species to Form Varieties: And on the Perpetuation of Varieties and Species by Natural Means of Selection." *Journal of the Proceedings of the Linnean Society of London (Zoology)* 3 (August 20, 1858): 46-50.

Darwin Correspondence Project Database. "Darwin's Reading Notebooks." University of Cambridge.

http://www.darwinproject.ac.uk/ darwins-reading-notebooks (accessed June 1, 2010).

———. "Letter no. 487 – Herbert, J. M. to Darwin, C. R., 13 Jan [1839]." University of Cambridge. http://www.darwinproject.ac.uk/entry-487 (accessed May 3, 2010).

———. "Letter no. 279 – Darwin, C. R. to Hooker, J. D. 11 Jan [1844]." University of Cambridge. http://www.darwinproject.ac.uk/entry-487 (accessed May 3, 2010).

Darwin, Emma Wedgwood. *Emma Darwin, a Century of Family Letters, 1792-1896* [Edited by Henrietta Emma Litchfield]. London: J. Murray, 1915.

Darwin, Erasmus. *Zoonomia; Or, the Laws of Organic Life.* London: J. Johnson, 1794.

Darwin F., Darwin L., Darwin, H. "Coleoptera at Down." *Entomologist's Weekly Intelligencer* 6, (1859): 99.

Darwin, George H. "Marriages Between First Cousins in England and Their Effects." *Journal of the Statistical Society of London* 38, no. 2 (1875): 153-184.

Darwin, Leonard. "Memories of Down House." *The Nineteenth Century* 106, (1929): 118-123. http://darwin-online.org.uk/content/frameset?itemID=A224&viewtype=text&pageseq=1 (accessed June 1, 2010).

Desmond, Adrian J. and James R. Moore. *Darwin:*

The Life of a Tormented Evolutionist. New York: Warner Books, 1991.

Evans, John. "The Coinage of the Ancient Britons and Natural Selection." *Notices and Proceedings of the Royal Institution of Great Britain* 7 (1873–5): 476-487.

Freeman, Sarah. *Mutton and Oysters: The Victorians and Their Food.* London: V. Gollancz, 1989.

Galton, Francis. *Memories of My Life.* London: Methuen and Co., 1908.

———. "On Head Growth in Students at the University of Cambridge." *Nature* 38 (1888): 14-15.

Giblin, James. *From Hand to Mouth, Or, How We Invented Knives, Forks, Spoons, and Chopsticks, and the Table Manners to go with Them.* 1st ed. New York: Crowell, 1987.

Gilman, Sander L. "Darwin Sees the Insane." *Journal of the History of the Behavioral Sciences* 15, no. 3 (1979): 253-262.

Gratzer, W. B. *A Bedside Nature: Genius and Eccentricity in Science, 1869-1953.* New York: W. H. Freeman, 1998.

Greenacre, Phyllis. *The Quest for the Father; a Study of the Darwin-Butler Controversy, as a Contribution to the Understanding of the Creative Individual.* New York: International Universities Press, 1963.

Greenhill, Basil and Ann Giffard. *Travelling by Sea*

in the Nineteenth Century: Interior Design in Victorian Passenger Ships. London: Black, 1972.

Gruber, Howard E. *Darwin on Man: A Psychological Study of Scientific Creativity.* New York: E. P. Dutton, 1974.

Healey, Edna. *Emma Darwin: The Inspirational Wife of a Genius.* London: Headline, 2001.

Himsworth, Joseph Beeston. *The Story of Cutlery, from Flint to Stainless Steel.* London: Ernest Benn Limited, 1953.

Howells, Jocelyn. "Beginner's Booklet." National Button Society. http://www.nationalbuttonoi ety.org/NBS_Publications_%26_Forms.htm (accessed June 15, 2010).

Hubble, Douglas. "The Life of the Shawl." *The Lancet* 2 (1954): 1351-1354.

Huxley, Thomas H. *Evidence as to Man's Place in Nature.* Edinburgh: Williams and Norgate, 1863.

Kaplan, Justin. *Walt Whitman, a Life.* New York: Simon and Schuster, 1980.

Langmuir, J. W. *Twelfth Annual Report of the Inspector of Asylums, Prisons and Public Charities for the Province of Ontario, for the Year Ending 30th September, 1879.* Toronto: C. Blackett Robinson, 1880.

———. *Thirteenth Annual Report of the Inspector of Asylums, Prisons and Public Charities for the Province of Ontario, for the Year Ending 30th*

September, 1880. Toronto: C. Blackett Robinson, 1881.

Leon, P. W. *Walt Whitman & Sir William Osler: Poet and Physician*. Toronto: ECW, 1995.

Little, Bryan D. G. *The Colleges of Cambridge, 1286-1973*. Bath: Adams and Dart, 1973.

Lumsden, Charles J. and Edward O. Wilson. "The Relation between Biological and Cultural Evolution." *Journal of Social and Biological Systems* 8, no. 4 (1985): 343-359.

Lyons, Beauvais. "The Excavation of the Apasht: Artifacts from an Imaginary Past." *Leonardo* 18, no. 2 (1985): 81-89.

Mayr, Ernst. *One Long Argument: Charles Darwin and the Genesis of Modern Evolutionary Thought*. Questions of Science Series. Cambridge, Mass.: Harvard University Press, 1991.

Morphy, Howard and Elizabeth Edwards. *Australia in Oxford*. Monograph 4. Oxford: University of Oxford, 1988.

Nagel, E. "The Meaning of Reduction in the Natural Sciences." In *Science and Civilization*, edited by Robert C. Stauffer and Richard Peter McKeon, 99-135. Madison: University of Wisconsin Press, 1966.

Nation, Earl F. "Osler and Tuberculosis." *Chest* 64, no.1 (July, 1973): 84-87.

Oppenheim, Janet. *"Shattered Nerves": Doctors,*

Patients, and Depression in Victorian England.
New York: Oxford University Press, 1991.

Pasnau, R. O. "Darwin's Illness: A Biopsychosocial
Perspective." *Psychosomatics* 31, no. 2 (Spring,
1990): 121-128.

Peile, John. "Christ's College in the Years Preceding
the Entry of Charles Darwin." In *Darwin
Centenary Number.* Vol. 23, 197-208.
Cambridge: Cambridge University Press, 1909.

Petroski, Henry. *The Evolution of Useful Things.*
New York: Vintage Books, 1994.

Pitt-Rivers, Augustus Lane Fox. *The Evolution of
Culture and Other Essays* [Edited by John
Linton Myres]. Oxford: Clarendon Press, 1906.

Raverat, Gwen. *Period Piece: A Cambridge Childhood.* London: Faber and Faber, 1952.

Reader, W. J. *Victorian England.* New York: G. P.
Putnam's Sons, 1974.

Review of *Man's Moral Nature* in "Book Notices." *American Journal of Insanity* 36, no.
4 (April 1880): 530-533.

Shipley, A. E. "Charles Darwin at the Universities:
Edinburgh – Cambridge." *Christ's College Mag-
azine* 23, no. 70 (Easter Term, 1909): 185-224.

Shortt, S. E. D. "The Myth of a Canadian Boswell:
Dr. R. M. Bucke and Walt Whitman." *Bulletin
Canadien d'Histoire De La Médecine / Canadian Bulletin of Medical History* 1, no. 2 (1984):
55-70.

———. *Victorian Lunacy: Richard M. Bucke and the Practice of Late Nineteenth-Century Psychiatry*. Cambridge History of Medicine Series. Cambridge: Cambridge University Press, 1986.

Singleton, H. Raymond. *A Chronology of Cutlery*. Sheffield, England: Sheffield City Museums, 1973.

Stevens, Colin MacGregor. "MacGregor Letters." Colin MacGregor Stevens: Family History and Canadian Military History. http://bcoy1cpb. pacdat.net/macgregor_letters.htm (accessed June 15, 2010).

Thomson, K. *The Young Charles Darwin*. New Haven: Yale University Press, 2009.

Turner, Noel D. *American Silver Flatware, 1837-1910*. South Brunswick: A. S. Barnes, 1972.

Van Wyhe, John. "Darwin's Student Bills at Christ's College, Cambridge." The Complete Work of Charles Darwin Online. http://darwin-online.org.uk/EditorialIntroductions/vanWyhe_Christ's_College_student_bills.html (accessed June 15, 2010).

Vance, James E. *Capturing the Horizon: The Historical Geography of Transportation Since the Sixteenth Century*. Baltimore: Johns Hopkins University Press, 1990.

Whitman, Walt. "Death Carol." In *Leaves of Grass*, 38. New York: Smith & McDougal, 1872

ILLUSTRATION CREDITS

Frontispiece. The Darwin Family Tree. Utilizing data from Figure 5 in Atkins H. *Down: The Home of the Darwins*. London: Royal College of Surgeons of England, 1974 and from the Darwin Pedigree, Emma Darwin Litchfield H. E. (ed) *Emma Darwin: A Century of Family Letters 1792-1896*. In Two Volumes. London: John Murray, 1915.

Figure 1. Down House: Back of House from Garden with Trellises and Climbers, Summer Half of Year. CUL location-MS. DAR.219: 12.172-173. Reproduced by kind permission of the Syndics of Cambridge University Library.

Figure 2. Photographs Used to Depict Suffering and Weeping. In Darwin, C. *The Expression of the Emotions in Man and Animals*. London: John Murray, 1872.

Plate 1 with six vignettes of babies. CUL location S382.d.87.1. Reproduced by kind permission of the Syndics of Cambridge University Library.

Figure 3.   Two Ancient British Coins (Illustrations by Thomas Darwin, from "Coinage of the Ancient Britons at Down," 1869). Drawing by Catherine MacDonald.

Figure 4.   Charles Darwin on His Horse Tommy. CUL location-MS. DAR.225:116. Reproduced by kind permission of the Syndics of   Cambridge University Library.

Figure 5.   The Etruria Works on the Trent and Mersey Canal. Photo taken in 1898 by one of the employees. Accessed from the "Home of the North Staffordshire Potteries" website, maintained by Steven Birks. Copyright holder unknown.

Figure 6.   Exterior View of Charles Darwin's Old Room at Christ's College. From *Order of the Proceedings at the Darwin Celebration held at Cambridge June 22-June 24, 1909.* CUL location Cam.b.909.2.   Reproduced by kind permission of the Syndics of Cambridge University Library.

Figure 7. A Facsimile from Thomas Darwin's "Sheffield Notebook." Drawing by Catherine MacDonald.

Figure 8. Menu Card Used for the *Plinian Society's* Grand Dinner, 1878. From Ainsley, Louis. *Looking Back.* Printed for private circulation, 1930. Drawing by Catherine MacDonald.

Figure 9. Thomas Darwin's Admission Medical Opinions and Schedule No. 2: Information to be Elicited Upon Enquiry of a Person Charged with Being Insane (Under Sections 19 and 20, Chapter 220 of the Revised Statutes). Adaptation and drawing by Catherine MacDonald.

Figure 10. Dr. Richard Maurice Bucke. Photograph courtesy of the University of Western Ontario Archives, The Richard Morris Bucke Collection.

Figure 11. Mr. Walt Whitman. Photograph from the Library of Congress.

Figure 12. Playing Croquet in the Garden at the London Asylum. Photograph courtesy of the University of Western Ontario Archives, The Richard Morris Bucke Collection.

Figure 13. Portrait of Emma Darwin in Old Age, Seated and Wearing Dark Clothing with a Frilled Cap. CUL location MS. DAR.225:80. Reproduced by kind permission of the Syndics of Cambridge University Library.

Figure 14. Pitt Rivers's Collection of Australian Aboriginal Weapons. From Plate III in Fox, A. H. L. "On the Evolution of Culture," *Proceedings of the Royal Institution*, Vol. VII (1875). pp. 496-520. This was the published text of a lecture delivered by Augustus Henry Lane Fox [later A. H. L. F. Pitt Rivers] at the Royal Institution of Great Britain on Friday, May 28, 1875. Photograph courtesy of the Pitt Rivers Museum, University of Oxford.

Figure 15. Rudimentary Characters (Illustrations by Thomas Darwin, from "Artefacts and the Origin of Their Rudimentary Characters: By Means of Competition Between Species," 1878). Drawing by Catherine MacDonald.

Figure 16. A Pastry Fork and Dessert Fork (Illustrations by Thomas Darwin, from "On the Effects of the Increased Use of a Character in a Domestic Eating Utensil," 1879). Drawing by Catherine MacDonald.

Figure 17. Hybrid Utensils: (left to right) Olive Spoon, Ramekin Fork, and Oyster Fork-Spoon (Illustrations by Thomas Darwin, from "Hybrid Artefacts and Their Role in Our Understanding of the Evolution of Inanimate Objects," 1879). Drawing by Catherine MacDonald.

Figure 18. Sir Joseph Norman Lockyer K.C.B., F.R.S. Photograph courtesy of the Norman Lockyer Observatory, Sidmouth, England.

Figure 19. Mr. Samuel Butler. Photograph reproduced by permission of the Master and Fellows of St John's College, Cambridge.

Figure 20.   Three Forms of *Lythrum Salicaria*.
From Darwin, C. *The Different Forms of Flowers on Plants of the Same Species.*
London: John Murray, 1877. Figure 10, p. 139. CUL location S370.c.87.4.
Reproduced by kind permission of the Syndics of Cambridge University Library.

Figure 21.   London Asylum c. 1880. Photograph courtesy of the University of Western Ontario Archives, The Richard Morris Bucke Collection.

Figure 22.   Dr. William Osler. Photograph courtesy of the William Osler Photo Collection, Osler Library of the History of Medicine, McGill University, Montreal, Quebec, Canada.

Figure 23.   Charles Darwin in Hat and Cloak, Leaning Against Pillar. CUL location-MS. DAR.219. 12:28. Reproduced by kind permission of the Syndics of Cambridge University Library.

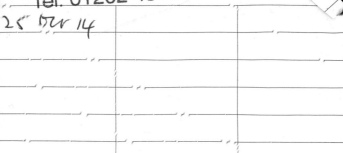

Castle Lane
Bournemouth BH8 9UP
Tel: 01202 451900

25 Nov 14

- You can return this item to any Bournemouth library but not all libraries are open every day

- Items must be returned on or before the due date. Please note that you will be charged for items returned late.

- Items may be renewed unless requested by another customer.

- Renewals can be made in any library, by telephone, email or online via the website. Your membership card number and PIN will be required.

- Please look after this item - you may be charged for any damage.

Bournemouth
Libraries

www.bournemouth.gov.uk/libraries